The Priestess and the Yōkai

Book I

Lindsey Merril

Prologue

Sesshoshi cut down another human bandit with his claws. The man had dropped to his knees and begged for his life. Typical. But Sesshoshi spared no one.

Bandits raided human villages along the outskirts of Edo and the western guard stopped them. Sesshoshi participated as part of the clean up crew. It gave him a chance to get his claws dirty. The blood running through his fingers didn't give him the thrill it normally did. It didn't feel like a run through a cold river, it felt like stomping through a bog. *When your reputation precedes you it is hard to surprise anyone,* Sesshoshi thought. Perhaps he was bored.

Sesshoshi flicked the blood off his claws. The bandits, the con-artists, the eta, and everyone in between knew who he was and they feared him. *I've become predictable,* Sesshoshi kicked the corpse at his feet. Killing was hardly fun if his victims always cowered at the sight of him. He needed something new to amuse him.

Sesshoshi studied the sun. It was the hour of the dog. He needed to fetch his younger brother and bring him home. Sesshoshi frowned, more human interaction.

It could not be helped, so Sesshoshi sped off toward the east.

Chapter One

Eiji hummed as she plucked herb after herb from the soft soil. She usually enjoyed her work but today she was restless. The wind was cool, the clouds offered welcomed shade, and yet Eiji felt stifled, like she couldn't take a proper breath.

She looked up to check on Lord Ko. She found him knee deep in the slow moving river close by, poised to catch a fish with his sharp claws. His white hair shone in the sun and his wide grin exposed his small canine teeth. Physically and mentally Lord Ko appeared to be four human years of age, but this would be his fifteenth summer. Eiji smiled. At least her mood hadn't touched her affection for Lord Ko.

"Lord Ko," Eiji called. The boy looked her way, his yellow eyes shining. "Be careful in the river."

"Yes Eiji!" Lord Ko yipped. He focused on the water at his feet. Faster than her eyes could follow, he struck the water and pierced a fish. He emerged from the river with his prize. In seconds he stood next to her, taking a bite out of his fish, bones and all.

"Yum," Lord Ko said in between bites.

"If you say so, but I prefer mine filleted and smoked." Eiji smiled. Lord Ko finished his fish and ran into the meadow to their left. Eiji returned to her work for a few moments before Lord Ko was back with a handful of flowers.

"What did you find?" Eiji asked. She didn't get much done when Lord Ko was around but she didn't mind.

Ko handed her one of the flowers in his hands. "A pretty flower. For you."

"Why thank you," Eiji said and tucked the flower behind her ear.

Lord Ko sat down, covering his white hakama in dust. "Tell me a fairytale!" He looked at her expectantly. Eiji glanced at the sun, it was starting to set. Lord Ko's caretaker would come to collect him soon.

"We don't have time for a story today. I'll tell you one next time." Lord Ko pouted and looked as if he would begin to fuss. Eiji bit back a smile. She had done the same when her grandmother denied her request when she was a child.

A pulse of energy rippled through the air. Eiji's breath caught in her throat. A powerful yōkai was nearby and it was approaching, fast.

She didn't recognize the aura.

Eiji gathered Lord Ko into her arms and balanced him on her hip as she stood. She turned her body to shield Lord Ko just as the yōkai arrived.

It was Lord Sesshoshi.

She'd never seen him before, but she'd know him anywhere. Her heart raced and she drew in a breath. *He's never come for Lord Ko before,* Eiji thought. Lord Sesshoshi, son of the western Lord Jou and Lord Ko's older brother. The villagers called him Regent Death because of his reputation for slaughtering anyone who merely looked at him the wrong way.

He towered above her. His white hair cascaded down to reach the small of his back. His yellow eyes were fixed on her. His expression unreadable. He looked as human as she did, except for his unique eye and hair colour that all wolf yōkais had... and Eiji couldn't ignore his sharp claws.

He doesn't look angry. Is that a good thing or a bad thing? Eiji wondered. She took a deep breath and regained her composure. She wouldn't disgrace her family by cowering like a mouse backed into a corner. She placed Lord Ko gently on the ground and bowed properly, dropping to her knees and placing her hands and forearms on the ground with her forehead resting atop her hands. Lord Sesshoshi said nothing. Lord Ko tugged at her arm when she continued to stay in the bowed position and Eiji took that as permission to rise. She met Lord Sesshoshi's stare with a respectful gaze.

"Good evening Lord Sesshoshi. Welcome to our humble village," Eiji said. She tried to sound calm but her voice wavered.

"What is your name?" Sesshoshi asked.

"Eiji, my Lord."

"You have a boy's name," he said.

"Yes Lord Sesshoshi," Eiji said. Her lips pulled into a thin line.

"Why would your father dishonour you in such a way?"

Eiji clenched her jaw. It would be her death to say something equally rude in return so she bit her tongue and tried her best to sound polite. "I'm his first born and only child. My mother died just after I was born from complications from my birth. He never wanted to marry again and he *really* wanted a son."

"Hn."

"Eiji, Eiji," Lord Ko said, tugging at her arm.

"What is it little Lord?" Eiji knelt down to his level. Lord Ko leaned in and whisper loudly "Do you think big brother will want the flowers I picked?" Eiji bit her bottom lip and glanced up at the opposing yōkai Lord.

Lord Sesshoshi tilted his head slightly.

"I think so, but why don't you ask him yourself," Eiji said. She wasn't foolish enough to presume anything about Lord Sesshoshi.

Lord Ko gathered the flowers in his small hands. "Would you like these big brother?"

Lord Sesshoshi glanced down briefly. He bent down and picked up the boy. Lord Ko grinned and put an arm around his brother's neck.

"Thank you Ko," Lord Sesshoshi took the flowers with every bit of formality that would be expected with the exchanging of gifts between Lords.

"You reek of humans Ko," Lord Sesshoshi said with a sniff, his nose crinkled. "And fish."

"I will bathe later!" Lord Ko laughed. He sounded excited. The comment hadn't phase Lord Ko but Eiji had taken offence. Her temper flared. Heat consumed her cheeks.

Eiji's palms warmed with a pink glowing light.

Lord Sesshoshi looked her way, his eyes travelled straight to her hands and then to the weapon at her side - the head of a scythe attached to a long metal chain secured at her waist.

"You are a priestess," he said. Eiji clenched her palms. By

letting her temper get the best of her, she had let some of her reiki surface. Reiki could destroy yōkai through purification. *I hope he didn't interpret my anger as a threat.*

"Yes Lord Sesshoshi," Eiji said.

"Do you think it is wise for a priestess to be spending time with one of the western Lords, especially one so young?" he said.

"I'm not a danger to Lord Ko. I would use my powers to protect him in an instant." Eiji narrowed her eyes slightly at Lord Sesshoshi. He could insult her name and her scent but she wouldn't let him imply she would ever harm Lord Ko.

Sesshoshi flexed his claws and Eiji's eyes went straight to them.

"Is that so?" He replied.

Lord Ko looked back and forth between his brother and herself. Eiji watched Lord Ko's face. *Poor thing. He can sense our anger,* Eiji thought. She tried to relax, for Lord Ko's sake.

"Are we going home now?" Lord Ko asked. Eiji wasn't sure if he had spoken to break the tension or because his patience for adult conversation had run out.

"Yes," Lord Sesshoshi said. He gave Eiji one last look before he sped off into the distance, disappearing in the blink of an eye. Eiji let out a breath and sunk to the ground. She had done her best to keep herself composed, but her heart raced and she needed to catch her breath.

Regent Death himself had stood before her and she had lived. Perhaps he'd been in a good mood today.

Once her nerves settled, Eiji grabbed her basket of herbs and headed back to her village. She weaved her way through the narrow streets. The merchant stalls were filled with activity. It was difficult to avoid knocking elbows with people as she passed. It grew quieter and the crowds lessened once Eiji reached the cluster of houses that made up Yamamachi's residential district.

Eiji's home was tucked away in the quietest part of town, far enough away from the rest of the huts to be considered isolated but close enough for her and her father to be useful to the townsfolk.

Eiji moved the shōji screen aside and entered. She washed her bare feet before slipping into her cloth slippers. The straw tatami mats crinkled under her steps. "Father. I have returned," Eiji said as she entered the kitchen.

"Welcome home." Hiroki fanned his face, the flies on his forehead scattered.

"How's grandmother today?" Eiji asked.

Hiroki let out a deep sigh and Eiji's heart sank. "She's as good as can be expected." Eiji frowned. *He's not telling me everything,* she thought.

"I'll make her more tea with the herbs I gathered today. Perhaps it'll revitalize her," Eiji said.

"She would like that, I bet." Hiroki said. "Is your little friend gone for the day?"

"Yes. His older brother picked him up." She gave her father time to process what she had just said. Eiji knew she couldn't hide Lord Sesshoshi's visit from him. Eiji hadn't taken notice at the time, but she was sure there were witnesses to his arrival. Word would spread and Eiji didn't want her father to find out through the rumour mill.

The exact moment her words sunk in was clear on Hiroki's face. All colour drained from his cheeks. "Lord Sesshoshi?"

"Yes."

"What happened? Did he say anything to you?"

"He told me to be careful of my reiki around Lord Ko," Eiji said. She didn't feel the need to tell her father everything else. "That's all."

Hiroki let out a huge breath. "Thank the gods you're safe."

Eiji nodded and bowed to her father before moving into the court yard to wash the herbs she held in her woven basket. Eiji returned to the kitchen to find her father preparing the medicinal tea her family had invented. Eiji's grandfather created the brew when he was younger and the recipe had earned him a living and a respectable reputation. Her father carried on the legacy and she would do the same once he was gone. It was a thought that once excited her and send a sense of purpose and peace through her veins but now it felt like a trap.

Eiji brought the herbs to her father and he nodded. She slipped the leaves into the bubbling water one at a time. While the tea brewed, Eiji swept the kitchen, sprinkling water on the dry ground to keep the dust down. Once the tea was finished, Eiji poured it into a clay receptacle and left to take it to her grandmother.

Her grandmother lived on the opposite side of the village, far from the other houses. As Eiji passed through the village, citizens moved out of her way. Eiji's white hakui and red hakama labelled her as the village priestess but the citizens didn't call on her often. They found her odd. Her time with Lord Ko, her boy's name, and her half yōkai best friend were enough to make her an outcast.

Eiji didn't need more work to do. She was glad for their distance, even if it made her feel lonely.

Eiji spotted her grandmother's house a little ways off in between the thick bamboo stalks. Her grandmother was known as the village crazy lady, so consumed with fairytales that she thought them real. Her grandmother's love of fairytales meant Eiji grew up listening to those stories. Those were her favourite memories. Each story danced around in her mind daily. *Too bad I can't visit those stories,* Eiji thought. *Maybe that would help my mood.*

She knocked on the cedar frame of her grandmother's home. "Grandma, I'm here with some tea." Eiji entered. She took in the sight of her grandmother. Her father had definitely avoided mentioning how much weaker her grandmother had become since yesterday. Her cheeks looked sunken and her hair had lost all its luster.

"Come in Eiji. Thank you for bringing tea," Her grandmother said. She pushed herself to sit using her elbows. "Oh don't look at me like that. Your father's pity is bad enough."

"He's worried about you," Eiji said. She moved a stack of parchment aside to make room for the tea on the floor beside her grandmother's futon.

"I'm going to die soon Eiji. There's nothing to be done about it," her grandmother said. "Why don't you tell me something exciting about your day."

Eiji told her grandmother about Lord Sesshoshi's visit, and this time she told the whole story.

"He insulted my smell and he insinuated that I would harm Lord Ko with my reiki," Eiji huffed.

"Of course he did. He's a yōkai. And he's a Lord. We're nothing but bugs to them," her grandmother said. "But he sure is handsome."

"Grandma!" Eiji laughed.

"You have eyes too, don't play dumb."

Eiji smiled. "I'm not blind but I can't see past his arrogance."

"Since I'm going to die soon maybe I should ask Lord Sesshoshi for a chance to hold his hand."

Eiji frowned. "Stop talking like that."

"Stop living in denial. Instead of frowning at me, read me a fairytale. That would bring me much more joy." Eiji sighed. Her grandmother read fairytales to her since she was a child, and her grandmother always read. *She must be really tired,* Eiji thought as sadness fell into her heart like a drop in a pond, rippling through until she could feel it in her entire chest. She knew her grandmother didn't want to see her sorrow so Eiji turned away to fetch a scroll. The hut was littered with them. Eiji had to be careful not to trip over one.

Eiji noticed a red scroll at the top of the pile.

She'd never seen it before.

Her grandmother's house was messier than usual, maybe the red scroll had been unearthed while her things were being shifted around. Eiji was about to touch it when her grandmother's voice stopped her.

"No! You must never touch that one."

"Why not?" Eiji turned to her grandmother. Her eyes were wide with fear.

"It's cursed and that's all I'll tell you. It should be burned when I'm dead," She said.

"Why don't we get rid of it now?" Eiji suggested.

Her grandmother shook her head. "No, I would be too sad to see it go."

"That doesn't make any sense Grandma."

"I suppose not but humour an old lady during her last days would you?"

"Of course." Eiji grabbed a scroll to the far left of the cursed scroll.

"Ah, Momotaro," her grandmother said as Eiji sat down beside her. "That one's my favourite."

"You say that about all of them," Eiji laughed and her grandmother gave her a nearly toothless smile.

"Did you know I've been there? To Momotaro's world?" She said.

"We all have, in our imagination," Eiji said. Her grandmother rarely mentioned the fairytale world, but the closer to death she got the more frequently she told Eiji about it.

"No. I was there for real." Her grandmother closed her eyes.

Eiji began to read Momotaro. She lay a hand on her grandmother's shoulder and pushed some reiki into her grandmother's body. Her grandmother relaxed as the pain in her joints and muscles faded away. When Eiji reached the end of the story, she looked down to see her grandmother asleep. Eiji pulled the thin sheet up to her grandmother's shoulders and took the empty tea mug.

She left to help her father for the rest of the day.

Chapter 2

Sesshoshi ran along the beaten dirt path with Ko clinging to his back. His bare clawed feet scraped against the dry ground.

His afternoon had been different. The kind of different he longed for.

Eiji had feared him at first, like everyone else, but when he insulted her she fought with herself to hold back her anger. It was easy to see the shift in her emotions, they ran across her eyes. He wished she had told him what was really on her mind, he was sure it would have amused him. What did not amuse him, however, was the feeling of her reiki rising to the surface and sparring with his yōkai. She would need to be more careful around Lord Ko. It was no problem for Sesshoshi to handle a flare of power like that, but Lord Ko did not know how to protect himself yet.

"Tell me Ko, why do you enjoy spending time with that human?" Sesshoshi asked.

"She's nice and funny. We play outside. I help her pick herbs and she reads me stories," Ko said. Sesshoshi could feel Ko burying his small nose in between his shoulder blades.

"Humans are a boring, constantly decaying species," Sesshoshi said.

Ko growled. "Eiji isn't boring."

Sesshoshi smirked at his brother's attempt at possessiveness. Ko's growl meant he felt that Eiji was his and that his older brother had insulted her, but he was no more intimidating than a wolf cub trying to snarl.

"We shall see what mother says about your continued association with her," Sesshoshi said. Ko remained quiet but the discontentment that radiated off of him was easy to detect.

They reached the western castle before sundown. Yōkai castles were much like human ones. The western castle was built on a high stone foundation. It had a white exterior with black

sloping tile roofs angled every which way. The interior was
sectioned into rooms by shōji screens and tatami mats. Humans
like to paint their shōji screens with elaborate scenery or animals,
often heavily accented by gold, but yōkai preferred simple doors
with their family crest painted only on rooms of importance.

Unlike human castles, yōkai castles were elaborate in only
one way: statues.

When Sesshoshi passed over the drawbridge, he passed
through the front legs and paws of a statue that towered over the
castle. A large white wolf stood over the castle, protecting it
within its stance and curling around it. The statue held the image
of one of Sesshoshi's ancestors that lived a few thousand years
ago.

Once they were within the castle walls, Sesshoshi set Ko
down. Ko ran ahead, his white hair jiggling with his uneven
steps.

"Welcome back Lord Sesshoshi." The servants greeted
him and bowed deeply. He headed straight for his father and
mother's chambers. Ko burst through the doors ahead of him.

When they entered the room, his father, Jou, looked up
from a scroll he was studying. He nodded his head slightly and
then returned to his work. His mother smiled brightly. Every time
she smiled she showed her elongated canine teeth. It made her
look like she was always up to something, which she likely was.

"Welcome back darling," his mother said. She bent down
and embraced Ko, her arms wrapping around him and enveloping
him in the silk sleeves of her kimono. "You stink of fish. Tell me
about your day." Ko needed no further prodding. He jumped into
tales from his time spent with Eiji.

"And then we picked herbs for her sick grandmother and
then big brother came to get me." Ko finished, running out of air
at the end of his story.

"Mother do you think it is wise to let Ko associate with
humans?" Sesshoshi asked. His mother looked at him. Her gaze
careful and calculating.

"Humans. They are something, aren't they? If I had a
choice, I would prefer that Ko spend his days with a tutor but he
gets such joy from his visit with this, this -"

"Eiji," Sesshoshi supplied.

"Eiji, hm? Anyway, I could never deny him."

"You are his mother. You can deny him whatever you wish," Sesshoshi said. He folded his arms across his chest, tucking his hands into the sleeve of his haori.

His mother grinned, showing her sharp canine teeth. "Of course darling. But what fun would that be for him?" Sesshoshi frowned.

"Satori, take Ko for a bath," Jou said. Satori nodded and scooped Ko up in her arms.

Once mother and child were out of the room, his father rose from his spot on the floor. "I do not need Ko listening to what I have to say next and then blabbing it around the castle for all to interpret."

Sesshoshi raised a brow.

"I know in the past that yōkai and humans have not gotten along. I do not think we ever truly will, but we must start trying to mend our relationship with them."

That surprised Sesshoshi. Though his father did not dislike humans as much as some yōkai, he was certainly not friendly with them either.

"Why?" Sesshoshi asked. Humans were weak, slow, and short lived. As a species, they posed no threat to yōkai.

"They are developing a weapon that can kill yōkai quickly and instantly."

I stand corrected. Sesshoshi's jaw tightened. "A weapon?"

"The weapon is in its infancy but the more the Emperor, the shogun and the daimyo associate with the barbarians coming from the west, the better their arsenal will become," Jou said.

"Why not stop the barbarians from coming ashore?"

"Doing so would put us in direct conflict with the Emperor. They already have this weapon and they would certainly use it against us to re-establish trade with the barbarians should we try and stop them," Jou said.

"So instead you want to build a better relationship with humans before they complete the weapon?" Sesshoshi said.

"Exactly. We have time on our side at the moment and they don't know we know about the weapon. I want our kind to approach humans slowly, instead of rushing to get on their good side once the weapon is complete. This will also give us time to think of a way to counter it if we fail to form an alliance," Jou said.

Sesshoshi nodded slowly. "And Ko? You think his interaction with his human will help?"

"Yes, my boy. Ko and his human found each other on their own. The timing was perfect really. Let him spend time with her. It would be wise for you to continue to fetch him everyday before sundown. Word will get out that Lord Ko and his elder brother are being seen in a human village, not killing and destroying, but playing," Jou said.

"I do not *play*."

Jou laughed so loudly the room seemed to shutter. "I would expect not." Jou returned to the scroll laid out on the tatami mats in front of him. "See you at the evening meal."

Sesshoshi took his cue and left his father to his work. He walked towards the dōjō. Thin paper walls were on his left and a waist-height railing lining the gardens in the centre of the castle was on his right.

Ahead he saw Ritsuka leaning against a thick cedar post. Her brown eyes were fixed on him. Internally, Sesshoshi sighed but his face remained as stoic as ever. Ritsuka was the daughter of the red panda clan of the north, the closest allies to his family, the wolf yōkais of the west. She often visited the castle and hung around, waiting to catch Sesshoshi alone. He was sure Ritsuka's mother encouraged her to do so, but Ritsuka herself didn't seem to mind either.

"Lord Sesshoshi, how nice to run into you." Ritsuka smiled, making the thick brown stripes running across her cheek bones wrinkle. All red panda yōkai had markings on their skin. Wolf yōkais did not, unless they were artificially made.

Ritsuka ran her clawed fingers through her long red hair.

"Greetings Lady Ritsuka. Visiting again?" Sesshoshi asked. Ritsuka grated on his nerves, but he knew if he insulted her, his father would shred him to pieces. The alliance between their clans was thousands of years old and extremely important. Neither of his parents seemed to care who he chose as a mate in the future, but they cared not to lose alliances to insults.

"Yes. I was on my way to see my cousin at the southern castle. I thought I would drop by and visit with your family. Your mother is always so kind," Ritsuka said. She moved closer to him but not close enough to be considered out of line.

Quite the detour, Sesshoshi thought.

"My mother enjoys your company," Sesshoshi said. He started to move around Ritsuka. "I am heading to the dōjō."

Ritsuka grabbed his arm. "I could come with you." Sesshoshi growled dangerously and Ritsuka removed her hand as if she had been burned. "Forgive me Lord Sesshoshi, I forgot my place."

"I would prefer to train alone. It is best if there are no distractions," Sesshoshi said. Ritsuka smiled brightly, clearly she had taken that as a compliment.

"I would not want to *distract* you." Her eyes sparkled. "See you around." She walked past him and continued down the corridor. Sesshoshi's shoulders dropped once Ritsuka was away from him. He walked to the dōjō and began to train, practising his stances and clearing his mind.

Chapter 3

In the evening, Eiji went to meet Haruka at the bathhouse. The air was cold and crisp and Eiji liked the way it felt to take a deep breath of it. The bathhouse was near the centre of town. When Eiji reached the entrance, Haruka was already there, waiting. Haruka was tall, like most yōkai - well, half yōkai, in Haruka's case. Her head reached well above the door frame of the bathhouse. Her eyes were more like her human father's, dull brown, but her dark blue hair was like her yōkai mother's.

"Hey." Eiji said.

"Yo." Haruka smirked. She pushed the blue curtain out of the way and the two girls went inside. The bathhouse was empty. Every night, Eiji and Haruka bathed just before the water was drained from the large tub. During the day the bathhouse was filled with women and their children, relaxing, gossiping or singing together as they soaked in the water. In the past, Eiji would go with Haruka during the day, but it became clear that a weird town girl and a half-breed were not welcome. The women pulled their children closer and old grandmothers spat at them. Once the townspeople had avoided them to the point that all of the regular humans were in one corner and Eiji and Haruka were alone in the opposite corner, Eiji decided it was best to avoid associating with them and it had been late night baths ever since.

Haruka placed her shoes on a wooden shelf and started removing her kimono. "How's your grandmother?"

"As good as can be expected," Eiji replied as she began to undress as well. She realized now why her father had answered her the way he did earlier. There was nothing more to be said.

They scrubbed and rinsed their skin and then slipped into the warm bath waters. Well, luke warm. The only thing that Eiji missed about baths during the day was the hot water.

"I have something to tell you. You can't tell anyone else," Eiji said in a hushed tone even though there was no one around.

"Who would I have to tell?" Haruka waved her hand dismissively. Eiji gave her a serious look.

"OK. OK. I promise on my family's honour and death by seppuku." Eiji smiled. A bit dramatic but it would do.

Eiji took a deep breath. "Today, I met Lord Sesshoshi."

Haruka's mouth dropped open. She sucked in a breath and Eiji knew an outburst was coming. She clapped her hand over her friend's mouth. "Shhh, remember I don't want the whole town to hear. Though they probably already know." Haruka let go of the breath against Eiji's hand. Eiji backed away.

"Fine, I won't yell. But are you serious? How is it that you're still alive?"

"I'm as puzzled as you are," Eiji said.

"*The* Lord Sesshoshi. I can't believe it. He hates humans. I can't believe you lived," Haruka said, then she gasped. "Was Lord Ko with you?"

Eiji nodded. "Maybe that's why he didn't kill me."

Haruka was silent for a moment. Eiji thought she might say something profound. "He's amazingly good looking. I'm so jealous you got to see him up close." Nope.

"Haruka!" Eiji's mouth dropped open. "You're the one with the death wish for even saying such things."

"If I said it to his face maybe, but not here. You have to admit he's handsome. I saw him at Lord Jou's birthday celebration. He spoke about three words and was only in my view for a moment, but that voice and those eyes." Haruka let out a dreamy sigh.

"Don't be foolish Haruka," Eiji said and rolled her eyes.

"Eiji! You'd have to be blind not to find him handsome. Stop acting all virtuous for once."

Eiji sighed with annoyance. Her grandmother had said nearly the same thing. "Fine. He is rather handsome, but I've been working very hard to keep those thoughts out of my head."

"Suit yourself. I'll stick to my daydreams," Haruka said. She moved over to the edge of the pool and rested her arms on the ledge. Eiji's eyes instantly went to the scar that covered most of Haruka's back. The flesh was bumpy and discoloured. Eiji narrowed her eyes. Having a boy's name might be an inconvenience but being a half-breed was far worse.

"Your mother was a raccoon dog right?" Eiji asked. Haruka nodded. "Is that why you're so dramatic?" They laughed.

"I was just noticing your scar again."

Haruka's face hardened. "Yeah. It's hard to miss. Those bastards."

Eiji nodded but she didn't say anything further. Haruka had told her the story many times.

The village where Haruka was born was not more than fifteen ri from her own, but they were far less tolerant of yōkai than Eiji's village. Most townspeople feared yōkai and distanced themselves from them, but other villages were violent.

Haruka's parents were considered an abomination by both humans and yōkais. Her father and mother were viewed as traitors by both their species, but they loved one another. Haruka's mother protected her family from hostile villagers daily. According to Haruka, her mother's family disowned them. Haruka's mother was killed defending the village from a yōkai attack. Haruka, her father and a handful of villagers survived the attack. Haruka was only six at the time but the villagers blamed her for attracting the yōkai. They beat her. Her father tried his best to defend her but it was futile. They beat both of them within an inch of their lives. They survived and moved to Eiji's village.

"Do you remember your mother?" Eiji asked.

"I have one memory. She was singing to me and putting my hair in a style that's traditionally worn by our kind." Eiji had only seen Haruka with that hairstyle once before, the day Haruka and her father arrived in her village. Haruka's hair had been in a long braid that would have reached the small of her back, but it was folded twice and held in place by red fabric and two silver pins that crossed over one another.

"What a nice memory."

Haruka nodded. They soaked in the warm waters for a few moments longer before leaving the bath. They dressed and bid each other goodnight.

As soon as Eiji returned home she knew something was wrong. The air was thick with sorrow. *Oh no. Grandmother,* Eiji thought. Her father entered the room, the sight of him confirmed her   suspicions.

"Father. I'm so sorry," Eiji said. Hiroki nodded. He looked ten years older than he had this afternoon. In his hand he held Momotaro, the tale Eiji had read to her grandmother. He handed it to Eiji, shaking his head. Eiji had never seen her father cry but now there were unshed tears in his eyes. He retreated from the room.

Eiji looked down at the tale of Momotaro. It was the last fairytale she and her grandmother shared. Eiji prepared for bed and slipped into a restless sleep full of dreams where she was part of the fairytales she had read as a child and dreams where she didn't have to say good bye to her grandmother.

Eiji and her father buried her grandmother at the hour of the ox. It was just the two of them, and Haruka. Eiji and Haruka carried her grandmother's palanquin covered with a cloth. The two of them lowered her into the ground. Eiji knew her grandmother wouldn't have wanted a fuss, she preferred dumplings over flowers. Eiji was fairly sure none of the villagers would have cared to help with the village crazy lady's Shinto funeral anyway. Their quiet remembering of the kind woman that once lived seemed fitting. Her father didn't say much but Eiji could tell he was hurting. Once her grandmother was laid to rest, her father went home and Eiji stayed next to her grandmother's grave a while longer before she could bring herself to leave and go to her own place of rest.

The next morning, Eiji found a sloppily written note from her father. Some of the ink had run from a drop of water on the parchment.

He had given her the day off.

Eiji couldn't remember the last time she had a day to fill with her own desires. She took the scroll containing Momotaro and headed toward the river. She was nearly there when a yōkai aura pricked at her senses. She quickly determined it was Lord Ko and his caretaker. Eiji realized she was slightly disappointed. *Was I hoping for Lord Sesshoshi?* Eiji thought, annoyed at herself.

Lord Ko's caretaker, a wolf yōkai, stopped before her. His

long hair was white like all others of his kind and tied back in the western style.

Eiji bowed to him and Lord Ko. The yōkai left them quickly. All of Lord Ko's caretakers left as fast as possible. They weren't subtle about their dislike of being in her presence.

"Eiji you seem sad," Lord Ko said.

"My grandmother died last night."

"Oh. That *is* sad." He thought for a moment, his brows pulling together. "What would make you happy?"

"How about we read this fairytale together," Eiji said.

Lord Ko grinned. "Yes!" Eiji scooped him up and they made their way to the edge of the river. Eiji sat beside the steadily flowing stream with Lord Ko in her lap and the story of Momotaro in her hands. She read it to him just as she had to her grandmother the day before. When she finished, tears were running down her cheeks.

Lord Ko looked up at her. "Eiji is sad again!" He frowned. He licked the side of her face with his rough tongue to get rid of her tears. Eiji laughed a little. The first time Lord Ko had licked her face it had startled her, but later she discovered that wolf yōkai children did this to those they care about, to offer comfort or show affection.

"Thank you little Lord," Eiji said. Lord Ko seemed pleased that he had lifted her spirits. She looked up at the sky. It was almost time for a mid day meal.

Eiji froze.

A strong yōkai aura approached.

She knew who it was.

Lord Sesshoshi.

He had come for Lord Ko once again, but he was early. Eiji's heart raced and she hoped for the sake of her nerves that this would not become a habit. Lord Ko ran to his brother, his hair a white streak behind him. Eiji bowed low to Sesshoshi as he approached them. She stood fully and tried to calm herself. Her eyes drifted to his hands. His claws were sharp and tinted red with blood. *He's been busy today.* Eiji frowned.

Lord Sesshoshi stood before her, staring.

"Can I help you my Lord?" Eiji asked. She kept her tone

even.

"How is it that Ko has come to spend so much time here with you every day?" Lord Sesshoshi asked.

"Uh..." Eiji tried to remember the story correctly. Lying to him, even if she had forgotten the truth, would be unwise. "It was about six moons ago. I was heading toward Edo on an errand for my father when I found Lord Ko crying on the side of the road. He told me he had run away but regretted it and he was too upset to find his way back. I recognized him instantly as the littlest Lord of the west. I took him towards the castle."

"I was worried that I would be killed if I showed up with him so I led him towards the castle and once the samurai were in view, I sent him on his way. Then I watched from afar to make sure they found him."

"And he returns to you? Why?" Sesshoshi asked. His tone seemed to indicate that this was the question she had been meant to answer.

"That would be a better question for Lord Ko. He found me the next day and has come every morning since. Lord Jou doesn't seem to mind so I do as the little Lord wants," Eiji replied.

"How noble of you."

She was sure by the disdain in his eyes that he didn't believe her intentions were pure. She couldn't blame him. Many people, human and yōkai alike, sought favour from both human and yōkai rulers to suit their own purposes.

"It is my honour to serve your family," Eiji said and bowed low. *And it's a miracle to stay alive this long around you. Now please go away,* Eiji thought.

"I see," Lord Sesshoshi said. It was clear to Eiji that he saw nothing, yet he asked no further questions. Eiji couldn't continue to worry about whether or not Lord Sesshoshi planned to kill her after everything she said. It was tiring to be so tense whenever he was around so Eiji relaxed a little. She let out a deep breath and lowered her shoulders. She found this made him a little more bearable. Nothing like constantly fearing for one's life to sour one's mood towards a person.

"Do I have to go home now, big brother?" Lord Ko asked.

Lord Sesshoshi folded his legs gracefully under him and sat in the grass. "We can stay for a while longer. Go play." Lord Ko let out a delightful squeal and took off up the grassy hill that lay before them. He rolled down the hill and then scrambled to his feet and ran up the hill to do it again.

Eiji stood beside Lord Sesshoshi twisting her hands together.

"Sit," he said. Eiji lowered herself to the ground. Lord Sesshoshi didn't look at her, he continued to watch Lord Ko with his sharp eyes. "Tell me priestess, are you properly trained?"

Eiji glanced at the side of his face and then returned her gaze to Lord Ko. "Yes. I was trained by my grandmother." A pang of sorrow shot through her chest at the memories that came to the forefront of her mind.

Eiji felt it before she saw it. Lord Sesshoshi shot his deadly claws towards her and Eiji blocked his aura with her reiki instantly. A pink light pulsed out of her palms and defected his hand. The way his yōkai pushed against her holy powers told her that he was testing her. *I wouldn't survive a full blow,* Eiji thought.

She looked at his hand. It was singed as if he had been burnt by fire. Her eyes widened. She had done it in self defence, but to harm her Lord would mean her death.

She looked him in the eyes. His expression told her nothing but his golden eyes danced with amusement.

"Do not look so concerned. I am not going to kill you when I was the one that instigated," Lord Sesshoshi said. "You are quite powerful."

Eiji stared at him for a moment before she blushed. "Th - thank you my Lord."

"Why do the townsfolk not ask for your services if you are a fully trained priestess?" He asked. Eiji's brows drew together. "You do not reek of the sick or the old. It indicates that you do not visit many clients."

Eiji smiled ruefully, but answered his question. "My father is an honourable man. He grows the herbs that keeps our village healthy. And I try my best to heal the sick. But the villagers don't seek our help because they think my family is -"

Eiji tried to find the right word. "Strange."

Lord Sesshoshi raised a brow and Eiji continued. "My mother died giving birth to me and rumour spread it was because my mother had spent too much time around yōkai. My best friend is a half-yōkai. My grandmother collects fairytales and claims the people from the stories live in a land of their own. And she claims she's been there. I have a boy's name. And I have befriended Lord Ko. The villagers treat me like I'm... *contagious*."

"I see," Lord Sesshoshi said and this time Eiji knew that he did see. Lord Sesshoshi undoubtedly thought she was strange as well.

Lord Ko rolled to the bottom of the hill and lay panting and smiling at the sky. "Lord Ko. Time to leave," Lord Sesshoshi said. Lord Ko gave his big brother a formidable pout but Lord Sesshoshi gathered his little brother into his arms without a fuss.

"Farewell Lord Ko," Eiji said with a warm smile. Lord Ko gave her a toothy grin and waved. She bowed to the both of them and Lord Sesshoshi took off, becoming nothing more than a streak on the horizon.

Eiji let out a breath. *Why? Why does he keep coming? Why is he speaking to me?* Those questions would have to remain unanswered. Eiji headed back home. On the bright side, his visits kept her recent feelings of restlessness at bay. It was growing dark. Eiji decided to retire early. She went to bed just as the sun set.

A loud crash in the middle of the night made Eiji sit bolt upright. Her mind was clouded with sleep, but she knew something was very wrong. The panicked voices of the villagers could be heard outside, loud and close. She threw her blankets off and scrambled forward to slide the shōji screens open.

"Yōkai! Yōkai!" The townspeople shouted.

Eiji threw on her red and white priestess garb and grabbed her weapon. She gripped the short handle of the scythe and held the chain loosely in the other hand. Her father stumbled out from his room.

"Stay here." Eiji told him before she slipped into the crowd. Eiji ran towards the east end of town. Clay shingles flew through the air. Fire sprung up from the houses that lay crushed at the edge of the village. A worm rose up from the rubble and Eiji's eyes followed it until they reached the top of the tree line.

The worm was huge and it was on a rampage.

She gripped the handle of her scythe tighter.

Haruka appeared beside her, bounding along in the careless way that her half-yōkai body allowed. "What a drag! I was having the most wonderful dream about Lord Sesshoshi. I saw you with him again today. We need to talk about that."

"Haruka!" Eiji hissed. "Keep your voice down. Right now we have bigger things to worry about. The town needs our help."

Haruka gave her a toothy smirk, her sharp canines showing for a brief moment. "I know. They're such hypocrites for it. They jeer at me and isolate you, but look behind you." Eiji turned her attention away from the rampaging worm and saw the villagers drawing back behind them. Eiji and Haruka were at the forefront and the villagers gave them looks as if it were all in their hands now.

Eiji huffed. "Oooh, those ungrateful jerks."

Haruka laughed loudly. "Tell them how you really feel, why don't you." She sprung up onto a nearby roof top and launched herself towards the yōkai.

"You know what to do!" Haruka yelled. Eiji almost missed her words as the yōkai crashed into another house, turning it into kindling. Eiji moved closer to the yōkai and stopped when she was in range. She let her reiki seep down into the chain until it reached the scythe. When all the metal was infused, she hurled the scythe at the worm. It hit and stuck in the flesh but the worm reeled back and the scythe came loose. It dropped back to the ground. The worm's flesh burned and melted off where the scythe had hit. The reiki that remained in the scythe leeched into the ground. Eiji frowned, that was a waste of her energy.

Haruka sprung and spun around the worm, tearing off bits of flesh and scales with her deadly claws. Eiji yanked her scythe back into her hand and infused it with reiki once again.

She waited until Haruka had the worm's full attention, then threw her scythe again. It pierced the worm's flesh, sinking deeper and deeper into the worm's skin as her reiki burned a path into its body. Eiji pushed more reiki down the length of the chain.

One of the villagers emerged from the crowd and joined the fight.

"Katsu! Where were you?" Haruka said. She leaped from her place atop the worm's head, running her claws down its body as she descended. She landed gracefully next to Katsu.

"Sorry. I didn't hear the commotion," he replied. He charged at the worm with his spear, piercing through its scales. Eiji and Haruka gave him looks of disbelief.

"Didn't hear it? You have to be joking!" Haruka's claws, like all yōkai, emitted blades of yōkai aura when she swiped them a certain way. Yōkai auras were was similar to reiki in function, but they were opposing forces − one meant to destroy the other. Haruka's aura was blue and it pulsed from her claws in narrow strokes that looked like shredded bamboo as they travelled to their target. The worm's scales flew off where the aura struck.

Haruka's blades of yōkai aura sliced chunks of the worms neck off. They fell to the ground in large clumps and instantly began to stink. Eiji covered her mouth with her hakui sleeve but still she coughed from the fumes. Katsu pulled his spear out of the worm and stabbed at it again. The wounds he inflicted were superficial at best but Eiji admired that he was part of the fight, not standing in the back waiting for Haruka and her to do all the work like the rest of the human villagers.

The worms swayed back and forth, spilling blood and bits of flesh all over the place. It was becoming unstable.

"Haruka. Now!" Eiji shouted. Haruka bounded over to Eiji and grabbed her around the waist. Eiji's heart jumped as Haruka sprung into the air. It was unsettling to be so high up. Haruka let her go and Eiji pushed more of her reiki down the length of the chain. Haruka decapitated the worm with her claws. It fell to the ground, crushing one last house under the weight of its body. Eiji fell and had to trust Haruka would catch her as she always did. Haruka pushed off the worm's body and intercepted Eiji before she hit the ground. Once Haruka had her on her feet, Eiji ran to the carcass and placed her hands on the scales. She glanced back to make sure that Haruka wasn't in contact with the worm in any way before draining the rest of her reiki into the body to purify it completely. The body disintegrated into a skeleton, the flesh burning off of it like smoke rising from a fire.

"They're much easier to purify when they're dead," Eiji said.

Haruka nodded. "Would have been much easier to decapitate too."

Katsu put a hand on Haruka's shoulder. "Are you hurt?"

She turned to look at him with a sweet smile on her face. "No I'm fine." Katsu nodded. Katsu helped them fight because he wasn't a coward, because he didn't discriminate against half-yōkai and strange humans, but most of all because he loved Haruka.

"Good work tonight. I'm off to bed," Haruka said. She stretched her arms dramatically above her head and yawned. Eiji didn't think she looked very tired.

The worm yōkai hadn't been very difficult to kill. There were yōkai like this one, weak and brash, that attacked villages for no reason; and yōkai like Lord Sesshoshi that were powerful and intelligent - they didn't rampage, they annihilated. Haruka and Eiji often had no problem eliminating the primitive yōkai.

Eiji turned towards home as well. It was the villagers' job to clean up the bones. Eiji thought it was the least they could do after she and Haruka had killed it. Eiji was starting to sway on her feet. She had used most of her reiki and it had drained her completely. As she turned to leave, her eyes caught movement in the treeline. At first she thought it was another yōkai, but she realized it looked like white fabric fluttering between the trees in the forest. *Strange.* Eiji looked again but there was nothing. *My mind isn't functioning any more,* she thought.

Stumbling back to her home, Eiji dropped her scythe and collapsed on her futon, not bothering to change her clothing. She heard soft footsteps and felt the covers being pulled over her shoulders.

"I'm proud of you," she heard her father say before his footsteps retreated into his own room. Eiji fell asleep with a goofy smile on her face.

Chapter 4

Sesshoshi had awoken in the night to his father's presence on the other side of the shōji screen. He sat up. "What is it?"

"Yamamachi is being attacked. We should assist them and make sure we are seen doing it," Jou said. *Eiji's village,* Sesshoshi thought.

"Yes father." Sesshoshi rose from his futon and dressed quickly. They took off together, moving quickly along the dusty main road that led out of Edo. Yōkai were like a strong gust of wind when they travelled. Sesshoshi was accustomed to humans gasping or startling when he breezed by them, but it was the hour of the tiger and there was hardly a soul on the road. The quiet during their travels was refreshing. Sesshoshi flexed and clenched his claws as they ran. He looked forward to having blood run through his fingers.

"What kind of yōkai?" He asked his father.

"Worm."

They arrived at the village just as the worm yōkai demolished one of the houses. Sesshoshi was about to jump into battle and tear through the worm when he felt Lord Jou's hand on his chest. His father held him back.

"Why hesitate?" Sesshoshi said.

"Look. The villagers are fighting the yōkai. I want to see how they do on their own. Just for a few minutes," Jou said. Sesshoshi turned his attention to the base of the worm's body. Three villagers attacked the yōkai and it looked as if they were holding their own. Sesshoshi raised an eyebrow. It was unusual for humans to do anything but die when a yōkai was rampaging.

"Two humans and a half-breed," Jou said. "Interesting. Ko could not have found a better village to associate with." Sesshoshi struggled to share his father's optimism. Half-breeds were a disgrace to their race, no better than vermin. That was one thing yōkai and humans could agree upon. Well, except Eiji. She seemed to have no end to her compassion and kindness towards creatures of any sort. Sesshoshi watched the half-breed attack the worm. She lifted one of the humans up into the air. He could see her clearly now.

Sesshoshi's eyes widen.

It was Eiji.

She threw a scythe attached to a chain at the worm and flooded the chain with reiki. He could feel the sparks of her immense power from where he stood.

"That is Ko's human, using her reiki to kill the worm," Sesshoshi told his father.

"I thought as much. You had mentioned she was a priestess."

Sesshoshi watched Eiji purify the worm. Once its body was gone her scythe had nothing to hold on to. She fell toward the ground with no way to save herself. Sesshoshi felt a strange surge of energy pass through him, wanting him to move forward and aid her, but the half-breed caught Eiji before he needed to intervene.

He watched as the worm disintegrated into a skeleton under Eiji's touch. Eiji looked up towards where Sesshoshi stood. He moved deeper into the woods, pulling his father with him. "We should remain hidden." He knew his father wanted humans to witness them save their village, but the job was done and Sesshoshi thought it would look more like the yōkai had stood back and done nothing.

His father gave him a puzzled look. Sesshoshi explained his reasoning and added, "Ko's human nearly saw us. I think it would be best to stay out of sight."

Jou chuckled. "Wise indeed, my boy."

Sesshoshi could still feel Eiji's reiki floating in the air. She was strong. Sesshoshi smirked, she might even be a worthy opponent against himself.

"Should we be concerned that Ko's human has the power to destroy yōkai so easily? She is very powerful. I have not come across a reiki this strong in decades," Jou said.

"I do not think so. She will be better able to protect Ko when they are together. She has indicated that this is her intention," Sesshoshi said.

Jou looked at his son. "What do you think of her? You have spoken with her. Does she seem kind?"

"Yes. She does." Sesshoshi glanced at Eiji once more before the two yōkai turned and made their way back to the castle. Sesshoshi returned to bed as if he had never left. His claws twitched. It was unfortunate he did not get to kill something but watching Eiji slay the worm yōkai had been worth his restlessness. Sesshoshi closed his eyes and slept.

In the morning, Ko woke Sesshoshi just before dawn. The little lord tried to sneak up on his older brother, but Sesshoshi could hear him coming from down the hall. *I will have to train him better,* Sesshoshi thought just before Ko pounced. Sesshoshi plucked Ko's leaping form out of the air easily.

"No fair." Ko pouted.

"I heard you coming. Should we work on that today?" Sesshoshi said. Ko nodded so hard his white hair shook around him.

"Can we read fairytales later?" Ko asked. Sesshoshi raised an eyebrow. Yōkai did not have scrolls that contained stories like fairytales. Yōkai were often the subject of them but they did not have their own. yōkai culture did have stories but they were usually about people who lived or had lived and what they had accomplished. Some battles were exaggerated, and romances were embellished but yōkai told each other the legends of yōkai, past and present, with a great deal of pride and fondness. Ko was becoming more interested in stories. He must have picked that up from Eiji.

"We do not have any to read," Sesshoshi said.

"Eiji does," Ko said.

"Perhaps we can borrow them," Sesshoshi said. Borrow was a kinder word than what he meant. If Sesshoshi asked for her fairytales, Eiji could not deny him.

Chapter 5

Eiji knew it was late in the day when she woke. Her reiki was restored but she felt drowsy. She pushed herself off the futon and stood slowly, giving her fatigued muscles time to adjust. Her eyes felt like she had stared at the sun too long but they settled the more time she spent upright.

Eiji headed to the bath house for a quick soak. It was mid day and the bath house would be less busy. Eiji would be fast to avoid subjecting herself to the scrutiny of the other villagers. Luckily, because she had just saved the village from a yōkai attack, the women and children in the bath house were kind and respectful of her. Eiji knew it wouldn't last but she was happy for the time being.

Once she was clean, she dressed and headed out to the herb garden. Her father was already working away. Eiji guessed he had been out there since the sun rose. He worked twice as fast to make sure they didn't fall behind because Eiji had slept in. Her father never complained about Eiji needing to recover her reiki but she felt guilty he had to work so hard for her sake.

"We're running low on achyranthis tea," her father said.

"I'll make more this morning," Eiji said. Her father gave her a look. It was well into the afternoon. Eiji smiled. "Right. I'll make more this *afternoon.*"

"Also we need to go through your grandmother's things," Her father said. "Tomorrow perhaps." Eiji just nodded. She wasn't ready for that but she knew he was right. Eiji helped her father trim the plants and remove the roots to be used for the tea.

Eiji felt that restless feeling creep back into her bones. The excitement of slaying the worm last night hadn't been enough to hold it at bay. Eiji frowned. What would make her feel better? She had no idea.

They were nearly finished gathering herbs when Lord Ko arrived with his escort. Lord Ko ran toward her in the blink of an eye. Her father flinched but Eiji didn't, she had grown accustomed to Lord Ko's yōkai speed. Her father dropped to his knees and bowed low.

"Good morning, Lord Ko," Eiji said. She nudged her father as a sign he could rise. Ko wouldn't do it, he was too young to realize he needed to.

"Good morning! What are we doing today?" Lord Ko asked.

"Today we're making more achyranthis tea," she said. Lord Ko squealed with excitement.

"He sure is easy to entertain," her father said.

Eiji nodded. "He's happy to do almost anything." She picked up the basket of roots with one arm and scooped up Lord Ko with the other. She brought Lord Ko to the cooking area of their hut and place him on the ground. Eiji cut up the roots. She handed Lord Ko a root every so often that he could break up using his claws. They threw them into a pot of boiling water and waited. Once the tea was done, Eiji drained it into a large pot, separating the water from the roots. When she was finished, she looked down to find Lord Ko missing. She turned frantically, trying to locate him and sighed with relief when she spotted him by the door. *Lord Sesshoshi would have my head if I lost Lord Ko,* Eiji thought.

Lord Sesshoshi hadn't come with Lord Ko this morning. Eiji tried to push the disappointed feeling in her gut away. She washed her hands and walked to the cedar door frame where Lord Ko was watching something outside. His golden eyes were fixed on a circle of children playing a game. Eiji recognized it instantly.

Lord Ko tugged as Eiji's kimono. "What are they playing?"

"A game. It's called Kagome Kagome," Eiji said. "One person stands in the middle and covers their eyes while the others walk in a circle and sing the Kagome Kagome song. Then the person with their eyes closed has to guess who's behind them when the song ends."

Lord Ko pointed at them, his little fingers bouncing excitedly. "I want to play."

"Alright. We can ask them if you can join in," Eiji said. She wasn't hopeful the other children would want to play with Lord Ko, but she had to try and accommodate his request. What Lord Ko wanted, he must get. In many ways Eiji was subject to

Lord Ko's whims too, but luckily for her he was a gentle and patient child and easy to guide from one activity to another. Eiji walked with Lord Ko over to the children. When they saw him coming, they broke apart. They looked ready to take off.

"Lord Ko would like to play. Can he join you?" Eiji asked. The children looked back and forth between one another. They seemed to know they couldn't deny Lord Ko either, no matter how afraid they were.

"Yes," said the tallest child. Lord Ko smiled bright, his long canine teeth showing.

"Don't cheat Lord Ko," Eiji said. "Your yōkai senses are much stronger than humans."

"Yes Eiji," Lord Ko said and ran into the middle of the circle.

Eiji reached out her hand to him. "Play once with me so you know what to do." Lord Ko blushed and joined her without a word. The tallest child stood in the middle of the circle.

They sang the haunting melody and circled the boy in the middle.

Kagome, kagome
The bird in the cage,
When, oh when will it come out
In the night of dawn
The crane and turtle slipped
Who is behind you now?

They stopped. The boy was quiet for a moment and then said "Yuji!" The boy called Yuji, standing in front of the tallest boy, laughed and shook his head. "Wrong!" The tallest boy frowned and left the circle.

"My turn!" Lord Ko said and ran into the middle. Eiji asked the children to tell Lord Ko their names before they began the game. Once he was certain he could remember them all Eiji reminded him not to cheat. They sang again.

When they stopped, Lord Ko called out "Jun," the name of the tallest boy. He was right. *He was probably cheating,* Eiji thought with a small smile on her face.

"Now you play Eiji," Lord Ko said. Eiji stepped into the circle and placed her hands over her eyes. The children sang. The song had a hypnotic rhythm that made it easy to feel disorientated. The song always made her feel unsettled. It felt like it was unfinished and wanted to say more, like it needed more time to tell its story.

The children sang and circled around her but Eiji could keep track of them easily by tapping into her reiki. *Now I'm the one cheating.*

Eiji felt a strong yōkai approaching them.

Who is behind you now?

"Lord Sesshoshi." Eijji took her hands away from her eyes and turned to face him. He stood behind Lord Ko, who had been the one that was actually behind her in the game.

Lord Ko turned around as well. "Big brother!" He hugged Lord Sesshoshi's legs. The other children scattered as quickly as their legs could carry them, some tripped and slipped in the process. Lord Ko looked around, confused by their departure. Eiji's heart ached for him at that moment. Everyone around them started staring. It was obvious the villagers were petrified of him.

"Let's go play in the flower fields. What do you think, Lord Ko?" Eiji said.

"Yes!" He said and detached himself from his brother's legs. He took off at yōkai speed to the flower field behind Eiji's house. Eiji and Lord Sesshoshi followed behind him. Once they stood at the edge of the field Eiji felt more relaxed. It was harder to feel the discomfort radiating off of the villagers from here.

Eiji bowed low to Lord Sesshoshi. "You honour us with your presence Lord Sesshoshi. Have you come to fetch Lord Ko?"

"Ko enjoyed the story you read to him the other day. You will provide me with all that you have in your possession," Sesshoshi ordered.

What? Eiji's temper flared and she gritted her teeth. It was so out of the blue. He was demanding that she give up priceless family heirlooms. Her grandmother had just been laid to rest, there was no way she would simply hand over all the scrolls her family owned.

"Those are very important to my family. They have sentimental value," Eiji bit out. She didn't care if it cost her her head, she wouldn't give up those scrolls so easily. "Would you perhaps consider having them copied for Lord Ko so that we may keep the originals?" She tried to contain her anger but it rattled around in her heart. When she met Lord Sesshoshi's eyes she could have sworn he looked amused. That only made her more furious. *My feelings are not a toy,* Eiji clenched her jaw.

"Very well. I'll send a scribe tomorrow," he said. Eiji opened her mouth to object but closed it. She felt as if she had already pushed her luck by her request.

"What is it?" Lord Sesshoshi said. It surprised her that he had asked.

"It's just, I still need to clean out my grandmother's home. The scrolls are a mess. I was going to do that tomorrow," Eiji said.

Lord Sesshoshi tilted his head to the side, studying her. "Very well. I'll send the scribe the day after tomorrow."

"Thank you Lord Sesshoshi." Eiji bowed low.

"Let's go Lord Ko," Lord Sesshoshi said. Lord Ko responded immediately and ran over to his brother. Lord Sesshoshi picked up the boy and they sped off into the distance. Eiji let out a huge sigh, she felt exhausted.

The next day, Eiji felt recharged and went straight to her grandmother's house at the edge of the village. She paused at the door. Taking a deep breath, she entered the house. It still smelled like her grandmother. Eiji's heart twisted in her chest. She wanted to curl up on her grandmother's futon and sleep surrounded by her scent. Eiji knew it was unwise to dwell in her loss so she began to sort through the scrolls, placing them in order. Eiji picked up The Tale of the Bamboo Cutter's Daughter. Her grandmother had said that this story had the best characters. *She also said she had met them personally,* Eiji smiled to herself. She had never been sure if her grandmother was telling the truth or if she had been beginning to go crazy with age. Eiji rolled up the scroll and placed it with the others.

She felt Lord Sesshoshi's aura near by. Eiji stood up straighter. Moments later, he swept into the room. Eiji jumped and turned to face him, bowing low as soon as she saw him.

"You startled me," she said. She clapped her hand over her mouth. "I apologize for my rudeness Lord Sesshoshi." He didn't seem to care. The look in his eyes remained the same.

"How far have you come with organizing the stories?" Lord Sesshoshi asked. *Always straight to the point,* Eiji thought and resisted the urge to huff at him.

"I just started. My apologies," Eiji said.

Sesshoshi moved around the room, looking at the various scrolls. "Your grandmother was quite the collector."

"She loved stories," Eiji said, moving another scroll – Hanasaka Jii-san – into a pile. "She even believed the characters were real. She said she'd gone to the fairytale world and met them," Eiji said though she doubted he was interested.

"There are legends of such things," Sesshoshi said.

Eiji's brows rose. "Interesting." Eiji's heart lifted at the thought that her grandmother may not have been lying, or crazy after all.

She looked up and her eyes widened. Lord Sesshoshi was reaching for the red scroll – the cursed scroll. The scroll that her grandmother had yelled at her for almost touching.

"No! Don't touch it!" Eiji said. She dove across the pile of papers to reach for his arm, but she grabbed the scroll instead. Just as Lord Sesshoshi's hand wrapped around it, Eiji's did too. There was a blinding flash of light and Eiji felt herself being pulled in. They both disappeared from the room.

Eiji hit the ground with a hard thud. "Ouch." At first everything around her was bright and blinding, then darkness enveloped them like a flower in reverse bloom. Eiji pushed herself up. She could hear Lord Sesshoshi moving to stand next to her. Darkness surrounded them. Eiji reached her arms up and she came into contact with a rough surface. She could hardly see Lord Sesshoshi but she was sure the roof of wherever they were brushed the top of his head.

He turned to her, golden eyes glowing in the darkness. "Where are we? What have you done?" He grabbed her arm.

Hard.

"I didn't *do* anything. I don't know what's going on." Eiji flinched away from his touch. His tight grip on her arm should have caused her pain but it didn't. Eiji only felt the pressure and the heat of his hand. She looked down at his grip on her arm, his claws dug into her skin. *It doesn't hurt.* Eiji started wide eyed at his hand.

"What is it?" Lord Sesshoshi demanded, seemingly annoyed by her distracted state.

"It doesn't hurt," Eiji said.

"What do you mean?" Sesshoshi asked.

"Your grip. I should be in pain right now but I'm not," Eiji said. Lord Sesshoshi let go of her arm. Her eyes had adjusted to the dark and she could make out Lord Sesshoshi's hand as he swiped his claws at her flesh. They slashed her skin but she didn't bleed. There was no pain either.

"I don't feel any pain," Eiji said, nearly gasping. "You can't hurt me." Then a realization hit her. "You tried to cut me!"

"It was a test," Lord Sesshoshi said. "And watch your tone. Think of who you are speaking to."

Eiji frowned. *A test. My arm is not a test piece.* Eiji backed away from him but she hit the rough wall behind her after a couple of steps. She ran her hands along the walls, they curved away from her on either side.

"I think we're in some sort of round – uh, something," Eiji said.

"Yes. I can see that," Lord Sesshoshi said.

"You can? It's so dark in here."

"Yōkai vision is better than human vision," Lord Sesshoshi said. Eiji huffed, of course it was. The ground shook and Eiji lost her balance. She dropped to the floor, moving her scythe out of the way so she could sit comfortably. The ground continued to sway. *It feels like we're moving on water,* Eiji thought. She sat with her legs folded beneath her, thinking it better that she not attempt to stand until the floor was more stable. Lord Sesshoshi stood solid as an oak tree. It annoyed her.

A bump shook the whole room and then the water-like motion ceased. It felt as if they were moving upwards. The motion reminded Eiji of when her scythe had become stuck in a dragonfly yōkai and it took off, pulling her into the air with it.

A feminine voice spoke. It was muffled by the walls of what ever it was they were stuck in. Eiji couldn't make out what the voice was saying. The room shook again and then bobbed repeatedly – *like someone walking,* Eiji thought.

"What do you think is happening?" Eiji asked.

"It feels as if we are being carried." Just as he spoke, there was another bump and all motion ceased. Two muffled voices chattered back and forth.

"Can you hear what they're saying?" Eiji asked.

"Not if you talk," Lord Sesshoshi said. Eiji glared at him.

"Let's cut it open with a knife," said the feminine voice. Two taps above her made Eiji cover her ears. Then it was quiet for a moment.

"A knife? What if they hit us. Get us out of here! Use your claws or something," Eiji said.

Lord Sesshoshi sighed but swiped his claws at the roof above them, releasing blades of his yōkai aura. The room split open and the walls fell away.

"Oh my! A little boy!" A voice boomed from above them. Eiji looked up to see a huge elderly couple peering down at them. Actually, they were a regularly sized elderly couple, it was Eiji and Lord Sesshoshi that were small. Two halves of a peach lay next to them, split from Lord Sesshoshi's claws.

"A little boy inside the peach! How marvellous!" The old man said. Eiji hardly had time to contemplate what they were talking about before her body started to grow. She became the full sized version of herself in a matter of seconds. Lord Sesshoshi stood beside her at his full height as well. *Too bad he hadn't stayed small,* Eiji thought.

"What have you done to us? Where are we?" Lord Sesshoshi asked the elderly pair. They looked only at Eiji.

"Wow he grows so fast! What an amazing boy the heavens have sent us," The old lady said, looking at Eiji. Lord Sesshoshi took a step forward, growling. The pair didn't react to him.

"I don't think they can see you," Eiji said.

The old man looked confused and exchanged a glance with his wife. "See who dear boy?"

"The yōkai Lord standing next to me," Eiji said. "I also don't think you can see that I'm a girl." Eiji scowled. She already had a boy's name and now she had apparently become one as well.

"Yōkai Lord? A girl?" the old woman said. "Oh no."

"I see what's happened here," the old man said.

"I don't," Eiji said, folding her arms over her chest. Lord Sesshoshi growled again.

"We don't get visitors often." the old woman said. "You can just call us Granny and Grandpa while you're here." *Visitors? Who are these people?* Eiji rubbed her temples.

A large bamboo tree to their right shattered into several pieces. Everyone jumped. Eiji turned to look at Lord Sesshoshi. His claws twitched and a few bamboo splinters fell from them.

"Tell them that Lord Sesshoshi, ruler of the west, demands to know what is going on," he said. *So they can't see you but they can see what you do,* Eiji thought. Eiji bit her bottom lip, she didn't want to relay such a rude message, but she did so anyway, only a little kinder.

"Lord of the west you say?" Grandpa said.

"That's impressive. We don't get much royalty in these parts," Granny said. They were completely oblivious to the yōkai Lord in front of them, but Eiji could see him and how angry he looked.

"Please, tell us where we are and what's going on before my Lord decides to tear everything around us to pieces," Eiji said.

"Oh right," Granny said with a kind smile. "You are in a story. Can you guess which one?"

Lord Sesshoshi snarled and Eiji rolled her eyes at him. She looked at Granny's smiling face. *We were floating in water, inside a peach, and an old couple found us,* Eiji thought. She spotted a wicker basket full of wet laundry and it clicked. "I got it! We're in Momotaro!"

"That's right child," Granny said.

"How can we be inside a story?" Eiji asked.

"This is a world of stories and art and other things. Everything that has ever been created is alive in this world," Granny said. "This is Momotaro. The story of the peach boy. We live this story in a never ending loop."

"So every time the story ends it starts from the beginning?" Eiji asked. Granny and Grandpa nodded.

"An endless loop. What happens in this story?" Lord Sesshoshi asked. He had stopped fuming.

Eiji turned to him. "In Momotaro, an elderly childless couple find a boy inside a large peach. He grows rapidly and on his fifteenth birthday, a group of oni begin causing trouble. Momotaro travels to defeat them and along the way acquires the help of a dog, monkey and pheasant. He goes to war with the oni's and is victorious. He brings the oni's treasure back to his village and they live happily ever after."

"You remember every detail of the story?" Sesshoshi asked.

"My grandmother read fairytales to me since I was a little girl. I've read Momotaro several times. I read it to Lord Ko just the other day," Eiji said.

"You read him a story about a human boy that kills a bunch of yōkai?" Lord Sesshoshi's eye narrowed.

"Uh – yes," Eiji said and looked at the ground. "When you put it that way it doesn't sound so good." Lord Sesshoshi let out a sound that was almost like a chuckle.

Grandpa interrupted. "That's right child. We have said good bye to Momotaro several times and awaited his return just as many."

"Hm." Eiji remembered grabbing the cursed scroll in her grandmother's house at the same time Lord Sesshoshi touched it. That must be *how* they were transported here. "I think we came to this world through a cursed scroll, but how do we get out?"

"There is an exit," Granny said.

"Where?" Lord Sesshoshi said. Eiji repeated the question for him.

"It's in the central domain of this world. Through a red tori gate," Granny said. She picked up a stick and hobbled over to a patch of bare clay near the river bed. She drew a circle in the sludge. "The central domain of this world is surrounded by, well, everything. You typically find stories in the north. Granny drew a bunch of scribbles on the north side of her mud map. "And pottery in the south. Paintings in the east and music in the west." She added more scribbles around the central domain until it was surrounded.

"Clear as mud," Lord Sesshoshi said.

Eiji's mouth dropped open. "Did you just make a joke?" He didn't answer her.

Eiji looked at the "diagram." "What do you mean by pottery? Like clay Buddha sculptures. They're alive?"

Grandpa chuckled. "Of course child. It was created with an intent, a story, a personality. It lives as much as we do."

"What happens if the pottery is destroyed?" Eiji asked.

"Then it dies here too," Granny said.

"How do we get to the exit in the central domain?" Lord Sesshoshi said. Eiji repeated the question.

"You simply have to travel there. Once you reach the end of Momotaro's story a gateway into the Overworld will appear. Once you're in the Overworld you can travel to the tori gate," Granny said. "But if you try and find it on your own it could take years. There are short cuts." She moved her stick through the maze in the clay, and then cut a path straight to the centre.

"What do you mean?" Eiji asked.

"Moving through certain stories will move you closer to the central domain than others," Granny said.

"How does that work?" Eiji said.

Granny drew a bunch of short lines in the mud. "If this is our door." She pointed to a line far from the centre. "Then going through just any story might spit you out here." She pointed to a door that wasn't much closer to the tori gate. "But if you go through the short cut stories then they'll put you here." She pointed to a line much closer to the centre.

"Alright then. Do you know which stories will get us there faster?" Eiji said.

"That I do. You must go through Hanasake Jiisan, The Tale of the Bamboo Cutter, and then Kobutori Jiisan," Granny said.

She turned to Lord Sesshoshi. "Will we be able to remember that?"

"Yes. I have it in my mind," he said. The certainty in his tone steadied her nerves.

"Be very careful when you are moving between stories. There is a divide between separate creative entities and unfinished work. They are desperate for attention, manipulative and cunning. They will take you prisoner. Always stay focused on where you are going next," Granny said. Eiji nodded her understanding.

"How do you know this? Have you been into the Overworld?" Eiji asked.

"Absolutely not. We've never left our story, but you're not our first visitor. It has been years since we saw her, but a woman has come through here several times. She told us about the Overworld and her travels."

"I see." Eiji wondered if the visitor had been her grandmother.

"We should head straight for the end of the story so we find our way home faster," Lord Sesshoshi said.

Eiji was about to agree with him when she realized something. "Wait. Momotaro fights the onis on his fifteenth birthday, but the story starts when you discover him as a baby inside the peach. Does that mean we'll be waiting here for fifteen years?" Eiji asked. Her heart thumped in her chest.

"No child. Time moves much faster for you visitors than it does for the real Momotaro. In fact, I don't think you'll have to wait much longer," Grandpa said. Barely a moment passed before a young man came running towards them.

"Momotaro! You are so strong and so brave. There are oni causing trouble on Onigashima. Will you not do something?" the man said.

Eiji grinned. "Of course I will. I'll go fight them and return with great treasure."

"You're no kabuki actor," Lord Sesshoshi said. Eiji glared at him.

"Thank you Momotaro," the man said.

Granny pulled a sack loose from a twine belt around her

plump waist. "Here child, take these dumplings with you." She placed the bag in Eiji's hands.

"Thank you," Eiji said.

"Let us go," Lord Sesshoshi said.

"My yōkai Lord is eager to get going. It was surreal meeting you both. My grandmother read me Momotaro's story hundreds of times. I've always loved it," Eiji said.

"Take care dear," Granny said. Grandpa winked at her. Eiji bid farewell to the elderly couple. She turned and headed down the dusty path that followed the river. Lord Sesshoshi walked beside her.

"So we are off to slay some oni, but how do you expect to get to this Onigashima? Do you know where you are going?" Lord Sesshoshi asked.

Eiji bit her bottom lip. "I have a hunch that this world will look like it's written. In the story Momotaro walks and walks, acquiring allies along the way. I'm guessing that there will only be one path and it will take us to our allies and our island."

"I hope you are right," Lord Sesshoshi said. They fell into an uncomfortable silence as they walked along the dirt path. Eiji fidgeted with her fingers, glancing occasionally over at Lord Sesshoshi. The more they travelled, the more her feet grew tired and the more the silence wore on her nerves. *I don't know how long we'll be stuck in this world of stories but if he doesn't speak then it's going to feel like an eternity,* Eiji thought. She tried to take her mind off of the silence by thinking about her father and Lord Ko. Her disappearance likely worried them, but there was nothing she could do to signal them that she was alright.

"Lord Ko is probably worried about us," Eiji said.

Lord Sesshoshi tilted his head to the side. "Perhaps. He is still young and would have some attachment to us." Eiji stopped mid step, his comment catching her off guard. She kept walking when her senses returned to her. *He makes it sound so cold. Of course he would miss his older brother. He's only a child,* Eiji thought.

"If you have something to say, speak," Lord Sesshoshi said. Eiji looked at him with wide eyes. "Your emotions fluctuate like ocean waves. And what you are thinking is clearly written on your face."

"Written on my face? Fine then, what was I thinking just now?" Eiji asked.

"You were surprised by my response regarding Lord Ko's feelings. You think he should miss us greatly. Perhaps he should even cry over us," Lord Sesshoshi.

"Of course. He's only a child."

"You assume that yōkai have the same kind of emotional attachment to their kin as humans. Lord Ko may harbour some sentimental feelings because he is a child, but he is not as emotional as you think," Lord Sesshoshi said.

Eiji thought back to her time with Lord Ko. In her eyes he was as enthusiastic, inquisitive and expressive as the human children in her village. "Are you sure you're not assuming he is like you?"

Lord Sesshoshi growled. A sound, Eiji was learning, that meant he was displeased. "That is a bold thing for a human to say to the yōkai lord of the west." It was true. Eiji had been careful about what she said to him in their home world because she knew he could kill her and she didn't want to cause more trouble for her father, but here it was different. He couldn't harm her and what she said had no effect on her social standing.

"Well, you said you can read my emotions, so you would have known I thought it anyway," Eiji said. In this world they were stuck together and if he refused to talk then irritating him was better than hours of silence.

"Hn," Lord Sesshoshi said. The path began to ascend a gentle hill. At the top, the river narrowed and snaked by them. There was a short wooden bridge and on the bridge stood a dog.

"Momotaro, Momotaro!" the dog called out. *Oh right, that's me,* Eiji thought. How amazing! She had always wished she could live out Momotaro's story and now she was. It made her smile.

She stopped at the edge of the bridge. "I'm on my way to Onigashima, an island wrought with yōkais. They must be slain."

"Stop speaking like that," Lord Sesshoshi said. Eiji rolled her eyes.

"I agree! They must be stopped," the dog said.

The dog stared at her, but Eiji wasn't sure what to do next. They were quiet a long while, making Eiji feel awkward. The dog should follow her, but apparently she needed to do something or say something first. She muttered the line from the fairytale to herself "the dog agreed that action was needed, so he gave it a – dumpling!"

Eiji fished a dumping out of the sack hanging from her waist. "Here dog. It's the best in Japan."

The dog took the dumpling and barked "thank you! I will follow you into battle." The three of them continued along the path. They travelled in silence once again. Eiji was hoping that the talking dog would be more... talkative, but he was as silent as Lord Sesshoshi.

They continued along the path until they encountered a monkey. Eiji gave it a dumpling as well and the monkey joined them.

"I can't wait to fight some oni!" the monkey said, bouncing from side to side along the path.

Eiji chuckled. "I appreciate your enthusiasm monkey." The monkey was much more talkative than the dog and Lord Sesshoshi. However, Eiji discovered that the monkey talked about exactly what she would expect a monkey to talk about – nuts, seeds, fruit, the forest. Eiji enjoyed the lack of silence, but she found the conversation less than stimulating.

Eiji let out a huge sigh. "Sure monkey, insects are delicious."

"Do you wish to talk about something else?" Lord Sesshoshi asked.

"Yes!" Eiji said. "I can't take much more of this, but neither can I stand your silence."

"Momotaro, who are you talking to?" the monkey asked.

"Uh. A yōkai that's with me," Eiji said. Her face turned red as she thought of how ridiculous she must sound.

"Do you honestly care about what a talking dog and monkey think of you?" Lord Sesshoshi asked. How did he know that was bothering her? Right. Her face. He had told her earlier that her emotions were clear on her face.

Eiji thought about it for a moment. "Yes." She could have

sworn she heard him sigh.

The dog and the monkey exchanged a glance. "I see. It's one of *those* scenarios," the dog said.

"What do you mean?" Eiji asked.

"You're not Momotaro are you?" the monkey said, waggling his eyebrows.

Eiji shook her head.

The dog said "I knew it. We haven't had a visitor in a long time."

"When was the last time?" Eiji asked.

The dog and monkey looked at one another. "Probably about forty cycles ago," the dog said and the monkey nodded. That told Eiji nothing. She didn't know how long a cycle was relative to the time in her home world.

"She came alone," the monkey said. "Not with a yōkai friend."

"Friend," Eiji echoed in a hollow tone. Sesshoshi shifted beside her.

"I don't remember her name. Do you?" the dog said and the monkey shook his head.

"Momotaro, Momotaro!" a voice came from above them. Eiji looked up to see a pheasant soaring in the sky.

"Ah, the pheasant," Eiji said. She spoke to Lord Sesshoshi. "He's our last ally."

The pheasant landed. "We must fight the oni!"

"I agree. Here's a dumpling. They're the best in Japan." Eiji said. The pheasant accepted the dumpling and vowed to follow her into battle.

"Pheasant, it's not Momotaro this time. We have a visitor. Uh, visitors," the dog said.

"A visitor!" the pheasant said. "How marvellous. Perhaps she'll get sea sick like the last one."

"Yes. What was her name? Do you remember?" Pheasant said, turning to the dog and the monkey. They both shook their heads. Eiji frowned. A thought plagued her mind. If her grandmother had been the one in possession of the cursed scroll, would she have been the last one to visit this world? The thought of her grandmother running around inside the very fairytales she loved made Eiji happy. It was also a relief to know her grandmother hadn't been crazy when she told Eiji she had been inside the fairytale world. *I miss her*, Eiji thought.

The dog, the monkey and the pheasant had moved ahead, walking and talking in a lively way. Eiji smiled at their camaraderie, but it surprised her. In the fairytale, Momotaro and his three animal companions were great friends, but in this world the four of them would live this story over and over again. Eiji thought they would tire of each others company but it didn't appear that way.

She glanced at Lord Sesshoshi. His long white hair floated in the breeze behind him. He wasn't as tense as when he first arrived, but his arms were crossed over his chest, golden eyes looking ahead. Eiji followed the line of his jaw. Her eyes came to rest on his lips.

"You are staring," Lord Sesshoshi said. Eiji looked away and heat rose to her cheeks.

"You're awfully quiet," Eiji said.

"I do not feel the need to talk when you do so much of it," Lord Sesshoshi said. A different kind of heat rose to Eiji's cheeks. "Besides, what is the point in talking if you cannot be heard."

"I can hear you," Eiji said.

"I suppose." Lord Sesshoshi shrugged. Much to her disappointment, he said nothing further.

Chapter 6

Sesshoshi kicked the sand at the shore. They had walked for hours through the forest and finally reached the beach where they would voyage to Onigashima. Sesshoshi had endured the sound of animal banter and Eiji's questions. He had never been surrounded by so much noise. It was no wonder human villages were so loud if all of them talked *so* much and *so* frequently.

At the edge of the shore lay a raft tilted in the sand. It was meant for them.

"We're suppose to use that raft to get to Onigashima." Eiji looked from the boat to the ocean.

Off in the distance Sesshoshi could see an island covered in embattlements. Smoke rose from within the fortress. It was to far away to make out any other details.

Eiji stood watching the waves rise and fall, her shoulders fell with them. "Can we rest before we go on?"

"Yes Momotaro," the dog said.

"We will proceed when you are ready," the pheasant said.

Sesshoshi frowned. "You were asking me."

"Obviously," Eiji huffed.

"It would be faster if we proceeded now," Sesshoshi said.

"I know but I'm exhausted."

"I do not feel tired," Sesshoshi said. "Perhaps it is because you are human." Sesshoshi watched anger rise to her face and her struggle to subdue it. *Tell me how you really feel little priestess.* Sesshoshi enjoyed watching her get worked up. Instead of yelling at him, she sat down in the sand and moved her fingers through the grains. It was clear Eiji would rest even if her Lord did not approve. He could not make her move, actually he could, if he really wanted to, but he found that he did not.

After a short rest, Eiji rose and signalled the others to help her push the raft into the water. The water soaked her hakama and it clung to her slender form. He could hear her teeth chattering. Sesshoshi stood back and watched Eiji and the animals struggle with a raft for a short moment before he pushed it into the water with his toe. Eiji smiled gratefully at him. The animals piled onto the raft and Eiji tried to hop on after them. The weight of her wet hakama dragged her down.

Sesshoshi smirked at her helplessness. He had begun to notice that she did not think things through very well. He grabbed her hips to keep her from being pulled under by the waves. Eiji gasped. Sesshoshi lifted her into the boat with ease and jumped in after her.

The dog and monkey rowed while the pheasant dictated their stroke rhythm. They rowed for some time before the island was upon them. The dog and monkey beached the raft with one last powerful stroke. Sesshoshi leaped from the boat and landed on shore. He pulled the raft all the way onto land.

"Who's doing that?" the pheasant asked.

"The yōkai that is with me," Eiji said.

"Oh right," the dog said. "I had forgotten that we have an extra with us."

They stepped off the raft and trudged along the shore. Sesshoshi followed close behind them. A large gate lay up ahead and a red and a blue oni stood in front of it. They eyed the group menacingly, tossing their horned heads and barring their fangs. Each held an iron kanabo and wore identical tiger-striped loin cloths.

"We're here to take you down!" Eiji said. She sounded more confident than she should, Sesshoshi noted. The oni were at least twice her size. Sesshoshi was not sure why she insisted on speaking so dramatically, but the sparkle in her eyes told him that perhaps she found it fun.

The red oni laughed, clutching his belly. "You're going to take us down? Bah-ha-ha." While they spoke, the monkey and the pheasant moved behind the oni guards. Sesshoshi watched the animals slip into the fortress unnoticed.

"They're going to unlock the gate for us," Eiji said. She glanced up at Sesshoshi briefly. "Lord Sesshoshi, if it pleases you, will you kill the oni once we are inside?" Sesshoshi raised a brow. She was directing her theatrics at him now. He didn't like that. It made her sound like Ritsuka and the other female yōkai that tried to get his attention.

"Yes, if you promise never to speak to me with such fake sweetness again," he said. Eiji's eye's widened at his comment. "It is – disturbing, coming from you."

Eiji's cheeks flushed and she looked away from him. "Fine. No more acting."

It is too easy to rattle her, Sesshoshi thought, but he was pleased with her answer.

The gates slid open, drawing the attention of the two guards. "What mischief is this?" the Blue oni said. It swung its axe at the monkey, who dodged easily. Sesshoshi sprang into action, looking forward to having blood on his claws once again. He was bored in this world. Though his conversations with Eiji had been mostly tolerable, their animal companions were irritating and had wore down his nerves. Slaughtering the oni would release some of his tension. He used his claws to dismember and decapitate the oni. Their bodies fell around him one by one. They were easy prey. Normally that would not bring him much satisfaction, but his need to fight something was great enough that his frustrations ebbed.

Sesshoshi glanced back at Eiji. The dog, the pheasant and the monkey stood by Eiji's feet. Their mouths hung open, they hardly breathed, perhaps afraid that the oni slayer would turn on them next. Sesshoshi was amused by their fright.

"Is your yōkai doing that?" Sesshoshi heard the pheasant ask.

"He's not *my* yōkai," Eiji said and then nodded. "Yes, that's him. You all look pale. Surely this can't be more violent than usual. The oni always die near the end of the story."

"Not like this. This is a massacre. I suppose we kill them all, but we're sorry after. Sometimes dog breaks his tail because an oni steps on it. Sometimes I can't fly by the end. Momotaro is always bruised and bloody. The oni die, but not like this," the pheasant said.

Eiji continued to watch Sesshoshi decimate the oni, her brown eyes never leaving him. He was not sure what to make of her expression. It was obvious from the hard look in her eyes she got when her mind was wondering that Eiji had seen many humans die at the hands of yōkai. Killing the oni should not have much of an effect on her. She had killed many yōkai herself. Was she disgusted with him? Impressed maybe? He found that it mattered what she thought of him in this moment – killing, the most primitive and innate part of yōkai existence. It mattered and that was a surprising revelation to him. Opinions of others had never bother him before, especially not the opinions of human priestesses.

He heard her speaking to the animals. "I've seen entire villages slaughtered like this back home. When we arrive to clean up, it's already done, but the carnage is the same." When the last oni fell, Sesshoshi returned to her. There was blood all over his hands and on his white robes, but Eiji still looked at him the way she had before he started killing the oni.

"Done," he said.

"Let's gather up the treasure and head back," Eiji said. The animals moved, pale and wordless to their task, each disappearing to a different corner of the island.

"They're scared of you," Eiji said.

"I do not care," Sesshoshi said. *And what about you?* "Are you not afraid?"

Eiji shrugged. She looked into his golden eyes "What I saw doesn't scare me. I've seen this type of killing, killing done by a yōkai, many times before. What scares me is you don't seem bothered at all."

"Should I be bothered? They are not real."

"I think taking a life should bother the soul. It makes me wonder if you would care if it were a human, or a yōkai, a child or – what about your own family?" Eiji said.

Sesshoshi narrowed his eyes and he let out a low growl. "You speak too freely."

"You asked, but sorry anyway," Eiji muttered. She turned away from him. No one outside of his immediate family spoke so openly to him. He had killed for less. Sesshoshi was not sure if Eiji was growing brave because she was protected within this fairytale world or – no, Sesshoshi was sure it was not her safety that loosen her tongue. *She is just like this. Unaware of the dangerous things she says and what consequences they could have.* He flicked the blood off his claws.

The animals returned with a cart full of treasure.

"Where did you find the cart?" Eiji asked.

"Under the leader's body," the dog said. They all looked a little less pale now.

"Are the oni your friends?" Eiji asked.

The pheasant shrugged up his wings. "You could say there was a familiarity to our routine."

Eiji bit her bottom lip. "I'm sorry."

"It's alright," the monkey said.

They rowed back to shore. The atmosphere in the boat was far less lively than when they sailed toward the oni.

"We'll take the treasure back to your parents Momotaro," the dog said.

"There is no need for guests in this world to complete that part of the story to move on. We learned that the first time we had a visitor," the pheasant said.

Eiji smiled. "So we can leave? How do we get out of here?"

The pheasant extended its wing to the right and in the distance Sesshoshi could see a white, oval light.

"There is a portal there that will take you to the Overworld."

"How do we get to Hanasaka Jiisan?" Eiji asked.

"You will need to find the door," the pheasant said. "I don't know where. We've never been beyond this world. Be careful, that's where the unfinished live."

"Thank you," Eiji said. She waved good bye to the animals and turned towards the light.

Sesshoshi walked briskly past her. Eiji jogged to catch up.

"Let us move to the next world. We will be one step closer to returning home."

Eiji only nodded.

Chapter 7

They travelled toward the white light that would lead them to the Overworld. Eiji mulled over the battle with the oni. She knew everyone in the west called Sesshoshi Regent Death, after his name and his – abilities, but now she knew what that name looked like in action. *Their limbs were like beans during Setsubun*, Eiji thought. Blood and bits flew like petals caught in the wind while Lord Sesshoshi, in the middle of it all, moved like a storm. It bothered her that he was like that, that he killed and seemed to enjoy it. There was a longing inside her for him to be kinder and that feeling frustrated her. There was no point in wishing that he would change. He was yōkai, they needed blood on there hands.

Eiji felt a loss. *A loss of what? What were you thinking would happen between you and him? Hm?* She was human and he was yōkai. Any interest he showed in her was just her projecting her own feelings on him. And what were those feelings exactly? Eiji decided she was physically attracted to him. She couldn't deny that, but that was all.

It had to be all.

Her stomach knotted when she looked into his golden eyes. She thought about his clawed fingers touching her skin and shivered. Her attraction to him was purely physical. She could get over it.

They reached the portal within an hour. Eiji was growing tired again, but she thought better than to ask to rest now. Besides, she wasn't sure if this portal was permanent or temporary, and she wasn't in the mood to experiment. If the portal closed it could mean having to repeat the story of Momotaro once more. Something told her that the animals wouldn't be happy to see her and her yōkai companion back again.

The white light hovered before them. They stepped through it. Eiji squinted. Everything was white. Lord Sesshoshi growled. The light must hurt his eyes even more than her own.

The portal closed behind them. Eiji turned around to see the last sliver of sandy beach disappear.

Eiji looked down at the sack that held the dumplings. One remained. Eiji took a bite. *So delicious.* The dumpling had come with her through the portal. *Interesting.*

Eiji's eyes adjusted and she could see blue doors all around them. She approached the nearest one. It had *Issun Boshi* written on it in kanji. It was a door to a story, but this wasn't the story they needed to find. Looking beyond the door, she saw hundreds more spread out before them.

"Look at them all. This is going to take forever!" Eiji said. Her stomach dropped.

"Remember what the old couple said. Momotaro's story will put us closest to the next story we need to go through. It must be near by," Sesshoshi said. His calm voice made Eiji feel better. He was right. There would be no point in taking a short cut if it didn't make it easier for them. The door they needed had to be close.

A shiver ran up her spine when she heard a scrapping noise coming from behind her. Eiji turned to see a disfigured female body hobbling toward her. She appeared to be made out of clay.

"Please," the woman said, taking a slow step toward Eiji. "Please help me find my dog."

"Your dog?" Eiji asked. The woman looked like a human peasant, but she certainly wasn't human at all. Her skin was grey and etched with lines that looked like they came from a sculpting tool. Eiji remembered Granny had warned them about the unfinished works in the Overworld. This clay woman-like creature must be one of them. Eiji started to back away and the clay woman reached for her. An arm circled around her waist and pulled her away from the woman's grasp. Eiji was pulled against Lord Sesshoshi's chest, and the clay woman only managed to scratch Eiji with her broken finger nails.

Eiji gasped and clutched her arm.

It hurt.

These creatures were able to inflict pain. *Could they kill us?* Eiji thought. She didn't want to stick around to find out.

"We should get away from her," Eiji said. Lord Sesshoshi was staring at her arm. He glanced at the clay woman and swiped his claws. His yōkai blades cut her into pieces. The grey chunks lay on the floor for a moment before reassembling once again. The woman cried and wailed, reaching for the two of them.

Lord Sesshoshi scooped Eiji up into his arms and took off at yōkai speed in the opposite direction. Eiji glanced over his shoulder. The clay woman pursued them, but she was no match for Lord Sesshoshi's speed.

"I think she's one of the unfinished works that Granny was talking about," Eiji said. She shifted in his arms and tried not to think about how good the warmth of his body felt. Her throbbing arm was an adequate distraction.

"It would seem so," Lord Sesshoshi said. "And it would appear they cannot be killed."

"I guess that means your method of problem solving is obsolete," Eiji said.

"Say something like that again and I will drop you and leave you where you land," Lord Sesshoshi said with a growl, but he was smirking.

Eiji shut her mouth. They reached the door to the left of Momotaro. Eiji was relieved to read *Hanasaka Jiisan* on the door. Lord Sesshoshi set her down.

Lord Sesshoshi took her arm and looked at it briefly. "The unfinished works can harm us." He studied her arm, a small frown on his face. "Are you alright?"

Eiji blushed. "I'm fine." The blood was already drying on her arm. She glanced at the unfinished work in the distance, the clay woman was moving closer to them. "We should go." Lord Sesshoshi nodded. Eiji slid the blue shōji screen open. She leaped through the portal with Lord Sesshoshi close behind her.

Eiji stumbled into a small hut. It smelled like distilling sencha. In the corner, an old woman sat while a dog slumbered beside her.

The woman looked up and smiled a toothless smile at Lord Sesshoshi. "Oh, hello dear." She looked from Lord Sesshoshi to Eiji. "Has our neighbour come for a visit?" Eiji could see the disdain in the old woman's eyes when she looked at her. *I must be the neighbour,* Eiji thought.

"What is this story about?" Lord Sesshoshi asked, ignoring the old woman.

"Hanasaka Jiisan is an old fairytale. I often thought about it as a story of little nothings. It seems that you're the old man who is married to this woman and I'm your neighbour. You have a dog that you love like the children you never had." Eiji tilted her head towards the dog slumbering next to the old woman. "In the story the dog digs up gold for you and the neighbour, me, asks to borrow the dog, but it only digs up bones so I kill the dog. You bury the dog where you found the gold. Then the dog tells you, in a dream, that you should chop down the tree to make a mortar."

"You put rice into the mortar and it turns to gold. I borrow it but my rice turns to rotten berries so I burn the mortar. The dog tells you to take the ashes and sprinkle them on a cherry tree, the trees then come into bloom. A daimyo who is passing by gives you gifts because the flowers are so beautiful. I sprinkle the ashes on the trees and it blows into the daimyo's eyes so the daimyo throws me into the pit. I'm never allowed to return to the village again." She liked explaining fairytales to Lord Sesshoshi because his eyes remained fixed on her the whole time she was speaking.

"So you are evil and I am good?" Lord Sesshoshi said.

"In this *story*, yes," Eiji said, smiling. There was amusement in his golden eyes, Eiji looked away. She noticed that the old woman was staring at them in a very different manner now.

"You're not really my husband are you? And you're not our neighbour," she said.

"No. We're not from this world. We came from our world into Momotaro's story," Eiji said.

The old woman nodded. "And now you are here, taking the short cut to the tori gate that will bring you home." The woman nodded slowly. "We haven't had a visitor for many years."

"So we've been told," Eiji said. "You wouldn't happen to know *who* the last visitor was, would you?"

"I can't recall. I remember it was a woman," the old woman said. "But you all look alike to me." Eiji laughed. *I suppose we would.*

"How odd it must be, to see your husband's face and yet know it's not him," Eiji said.

"It was only frightening the first time, now I know he'll return to me when this cycle of the story ends," the woman said.

Eiji smiled at her.

The old woman gestured with her hand to the pot simmering over the fire. "The tea is ready if you would like some. The dog will show you to the gold soon, once he wakes up from his nap." She ran her wrinkled fingers through the dog's brown fur.

Eiji made her way over to the fire. She poured a cup of tea into a clay mug. "Would you like some tea, my Lord?" Eiji asked.

"Yes," he said, moving to sit across from her. She offered him the cup while bowing low. He took it from her, his hands brushing against hers for a brief moment. Eiji was grateful her head was bowed because she was sure her face had grown red. Again. *Knock it off,* Eiji told her body.

She poured herself a mug of tea. They sat in silence while they drank. Just moments after Eiji had finished her tea, the dog woke up. It shuffled over to Lord Sesshoshi and nudged his elbow. Eiji put her empty cup down. "Let's see where he takes us."

"Are you suppose to follow us?" Lord Sesshoshi asked.

Eiji looked over at the old woman. She said nothing, only looked at Eiji with a wrinkled frown on her face.

Eiji shrugged. "I'd rather not stay here. If the dog won't find the gold for you then I'll go somewhere else." Lord Sesshoshi gave a nod and they left the hut. The dog led them through the small village that surrounded the old woman's hut. The writer that composed this story clearly liked small, square homes with straw roofs. The village huts looked nearly identical. They walked up a large hill with a gentle incline and into the thick forest that lay at the top. The dog led them a ways in and then sat down at the base of a tree. It looked at Lord Sesshoshi expectantly.

Lord Sesshoshi stared back at the dog. "What does it want from me?"

Eiji really wanted to point out that she had explained the whole story to him already, but instead she said, "the dog is going to dig up a box filled with gold. That's all I know. Maybe he wants some encouragement?"

Lord Sesshoshi reached down and patted the dogs head twice. He straightened and folded his arms into his haori sleeves. Although Eiji thought his gesture was a joke, the dog seemed to think it was enough and started to dig. It uncovered an iron box and looked up at Lord Sesshoshi again.

Lord Sesshoshi bent down and picked up the box. There was gold inside. "She speaks the truth."

"I've never lied to you before," Eiji said. Her tone was more biting than she had meant it to be.

Lord Sesshoshi shrugged. "It's what humans do best."

Eiji's mouth dropped open. It took her a moment to think of what to say in return, but by the time her thoughts had caught up with her, Lord Sesshoshi was already walking back through the forest, the dog following next to him.

Eiji frowned at his back, but bit her tongue and followed him without saying a word.

Lord Sesshoshi took the gold to the old woman. Then Eiji asked to borrow the dog.

"The last visitor you had, did she have to kill the dog in order for the story to progress?" Eiji asked.

The old woman nodded.

"Oh."

"But thank you for asking." The old woman bowed. "You can bury him where you found the gold." Eiji nodded and left with the dog and Lord Sesshoshi once again. They walked back to the forest. The dog dug another hole and it contained only bones.

Eiji knew now was the time to kill the dog, that's how the story went, but her heart felt heavy in her chest.

The dog looked at her.

It knew.

Is it any better that he sees the neighbour's face and not my own? Eiji thought. No, it wasn't. Eiji felt like the dog's eyes pierced her soul. Eiji wasn't sure if the neighbour ever felt like this, perhaps his anger was enough to blind him to any compassionate emotions. She certainly didn't think this was a story of small nothings anymore. Even the oni battle in Momotaro's story had seemed less barbaric than this.

Eiji swallowed a lump in her throat. "I can't do it."

"Hn?" Lord Sesshoshi hummed.

"I can't kill the dog," Eiji said. When she heard a light scoff, she glared at him.

"The dog is not real," Lord Seshoshi said. "I will do it if you would rather not get any blood on your hands."

Eiji shook her head. "As much as I would prefer that, I don't know how flexible these stories are. If you kill the dog does that mean we have to start over again? You're the old man, after all, and I'm the neighbour."

"I know not what will happen," Lord Sesshoshi said.

Eiji sighed.

"I could guide your hand."

Eiji looked up at him. She felt close to tears so she only nodded. Lord Sesshoshi took out his long sword from the scabbard and placed it in Eiji's hand. He moved his arm past hers and closed his hand around her own. Eiji's heart thudded in her chest. She hadn't thought of how close he would need to be in order to do this for her. She closed her eyes, unable to look at the dog any longer.

"Relax your muscles," Lord Sesshoshi said. His warm breath tickled her ear. Eiji took a deep breath and tried to let her arm move as loosely as possible. She felt Lord Sesshoshi swing her arm with great power and force. Eiji heard the dog yelp and then a thud. She shut her eyes tighter.

"It is done." As soon as he said it, Eiji dropped the sword. Lord Sesshoshi's hand stayed on her's for a moment. Eiji continued to squeeze her eyes shut. She heard some shuffling and then the sound of the dog's body being pushed into the hole followed by dirt moving. Once it was silent again, Eiji opened one eye. The dog was gone, and a fresh mound of dirt covered the hole where they had found the gold.

"Thank you," Eiji said. She turned and headed back the way they had come. She didn't feel like lingering by the grave.

She heard Lord Sesshoshi replace his sword in its scabbard and follow after her.

"Does it really bother you so much? You have killed before, have you not?"

"I've killed yōkai that attack my village, but I don't kill innocent animals."

Lord Sesshoshi let out a disbelieving laugh. "You eat meat. How do you suppose that comes about?"

"Father deals with that. I -" Eiji knew she had lost. "I just – It just bothered me, alright?"

"Maybe you just wanted me to hold your hand," Lord Sesshoshi said. Eiji looked up at him incredulously.

"I most certainly did not." It was true. The hand holding was just a pleasant by product of an unpleasant act.

"What now?" he asked. Eiji was grateful he had dropped the subject.

"Now we sleep. You're suppose to dream that the dog tells you to chop down the tree we buried him under and make a mortar."

"Then why don't we just do that right now?"

"Honestly? Because I'm tired. I need to sleep and you need to dream," Eiji said.

"And if I order you to return to the forest as your Lord?" he said, looking down at her.

Eiji put her hands on her hips. "I'll sleep on my feet." She narrowed her eyes at him. Eiji thought she saw the corner of his mouth twitch up into a smirk.

"Very well then. Where would the dwelling of your character be?" Lord Sesshoshi scanned the village.

Eiji looked around at the various huts as well. "Good question." They could sleep at the old woman's hut, but it felt strange to sleep in the home of someone she didn't know. Her dwelling, the neighbour's hut, might have a comfortable futon to sleep on. Imagining a soft futon to rest on made her weary body feel even more sore. There were too many huts to search through. A young man walked by, with a pitch fork resting over his right shoulder. "Where do I live?" Eiji asked him.

The young man stopped in his tracks and looked Eiji up

and down. His eyes hardened. "You live over there." He pointed at a hut at the corner of the village, a little removed from everyone else.

"Thank you. Sometimes I forget, with my old age and all," Eiji said. The young man said nothing more before walking away as quickly as he could.

"People really hate you," Lord Sesshoshi said.

Eiji frowned. "I know. I'm use to people from my village looking at me like I'm strange. Sometimes they look at me like they're frightened, but I'm not at all use to people looking at me with such hate in their eyes."

Lord Sesshoshi chuckled softly. "I am."

"Of course people look at you that way, you're Regent Death," Eiji said. She slapped her hand over her mouth. *I can't believe I said that out loud,* Eiji thought. She met his eyes briefly and was surprised to find him smirking at her.

"Regent Death, you say?" He flexed his claws. "Who calls me that?"

"Uh, just me," Eiji said. She wasn't going to risk dragging anyone else into her mess.

"Just you?"

"Just me."

"I know you're lying, priestess. I've heard many people call me by that name. Plus, you smell different when you lie," Lord Sesshoshi said.

Eiji swallowed. "I smell different? Wait, I don't lie that often. How many times do you think I've lied to you?"

"You do not often lie with your words, but with your feelings. You usually want to give me a piece of your mind but you refrain." He poked her in the forehead. "Right now, however, you are lying outright." Eiji looked at the ground, tired of staring into his eyes.

"Do you all believe I am so fickle? That I kill so easily?" Lord Sesshoshi said.

"You're yōkai, a yōkai named Regent Death. You've killed many humans. I've heard the stories."

He narrowed his eyes. "Stories. Like the one we are in now? How do these stories paint me? A cold hearted killer?" He scoffed. "As if I would be so tactless as to kill for no reason."

"You've killed lots of humans!" Eiji said.

"Some humans deserve to die."

"Some yōkai deserve to die too."

"I know. I kill both."

Eiji frowned. Lord Sesshoshi pointed a clawed finger at her forehead. "You are doing it again. You are lying with your feelings." Eiji's eyes widen. Was he being playful? Eiji looked at him. No, he was serious.

"Why not tell me exactly what is on your mind?"

"I want to keep my head attached to my shoulders," Eiji said.

His eyes narrowed dangerously at her for a brief moment. "Again. I do not kill so mindlessly. Besides, I cannot harm you in this world. In this world, you do not bow to me as you would in our realm. You do not wait for me to allow you to speak. So why not tell me exactly how you feel? It is not any more dangerous than the behaviours you have already indulged in."

Eiji wasn't foolish enough to tell him everything on her mind, but she trusted him enough to loosen her emotional restraints, a little. "Fine. I can't understand how you can speak so casually about killing people and yōkai. Taking a life is serious."

Sesshoshi levelled his gaze at her. "Of course it is. Do you think that because I can speak about killing without weeping that I take it lightly?"

"I –" Eiji started to give him a piece of her mind but she found that she had assumed exactly that.

"You did. I can tell you that you are mistaken. I do not kill mindlessly like ronin or lowly yōkai," Sesshoshi said.

"I'm sorry. I shouldn't have assumed such things about you," Eiji said. She turned her gaze towards the hut they would rest in for the night. Lord Sesshoshi followed her gaze and began to walk towards it without saying another word. Eiji kept her eyes on the ground.

The hut was full of loneliness. It oozed out of the walls. It weighed heavily on Eiji's shoulders. The man, the neighbour in the fairytale, was a sad man. Two futons were folded at the back of the hut. Eiji handed one of them to Lord Sesshoshi without looking at his face. *Why are there two futons?* Eiji wondered. Did the old man have a wife? Did she leave him? Was she dead? There were so many details to this story that Eiji didn't know. She guessed she would never find out. *Perhaps I can ask the old woman in the morning,* Eiji thought while unfurling her futon on the floor.

Eiji sat on the futon with her legs crossed. She heard Sesshoshi shuffling close by and her cheeks began to burn. Would she be able to sleep with him so close? Eiji undid her waist-length hair from its bonds in the traditional priestess hair style. She ran her fingers through it and quietly hummed a song to take her mind off of the yōkai lord next to her.

> *Kagome Kagome*
> *The bird in the cage,*
> *When, oh when will it come out*
> *In the night of the dawn*
> *The crane and turtle slipped*
> *Who is behind you now?*

"That's the song you sung with Lord Ko," Lord Sesshoshi said.

"Yes. It's a game the children play." Eiji had always been good at it. Her reiki gave her an unfair advantage. She was always able to tell who was behind her and eventually the other children didn't want to play with her anymore.

"Not yōkai children," Sesshoshi said.

"I suppose it would be below them to play such games."

"Children are children regardless of the species. It is not a game we are familiar with," Sesshoshi said. "Besides, if the goal is to guess who is behind you, it would be too easy for yōkai to play."

Eiji laughed. "True. I wasn't allowed to play once the other children became annoyed that I always won."

"Your reiki."

Eiji nodded. "You know, I've always wondered about that song. There's only one verse. It seems unfinished to me."

"Hn."

Eiji lay back on her futon and stared at the ceiling. The sound of Sesshoshi's steady breathing unnerved her. She felt as if the room was growing warmer. *Don't be foolish.* She reminded herself. *He would never be interested in a lowly human like you.* Her exhaustion won over her nerves quickly and she fell into a deep sleep.

Chapter 8

Sesshoshi dreamt of the dog, as he was suppose to. He opened his eyes slowly once the dawn light spread through the hut. He found Eiji already awake and tying her hair back into its priestess style. She folded her futon and put it away

"Did you have your prophetic dog dream?" Eiji asked.

He looked up at her with a small smile on his lips. The way she phrased things was amusing. "I did."

"Alright. Let's get to chopping down that tree," Eiji said.

"Hn."

They walked to the tree where they had buried the dog. Eiji looked at Sesshoshi expectantly. He swiped at the tree with his claws. The tree broke into large chunks and Sesshoshi picked one up.

"Now we have to ask the old woman to make the mortar," Eiji said. Sesshoshi carried the piece of tree back to the old woman's hut. The old woman looked up and gestured to the empty space next to her. "Put it there. I'll make the mortar."

Sesshoshi heard Eiji let out a breath. She looked relieved that the old woman was cooperating. He found it strange that Eiji cared so much about the old woman's feelings toward her. They were just figures in a story. If the old woman disliked them it wasn't Eiji's fault and yet she seemed to internalize the guilt of everything they had done and would have to do as if she had a choice in the matter.

The old woman's skilled hands chipped away at the wood.

"Do you know what happened to your neighbour – uh, me – to make him so bitter? There's two futons in the hut but he lives alone," Eiji asked. Sesshoshi glanced at her with a raised brow, but he said nothing. He had also noticed the extra futon, but had thought no further than the convenience of it.

The old woman didn't look up from her carving. "I know what happened." She laughed darkly to herself. "That man has two problems. He values money more than anything else."

"Do not all humans?" Sesshoshi said.

"Not *all* of us," Eiji huffed. "Yōkai must value it equally as much considering how much they charge us for things."

"It is not because we value it. It is a game we play with your kind." Eiji's mouth dropped open at the admission. She was about to say more but a chuckle from the old woman stopped her.

Both Sesshoshi and Eiji looked at her. "I would love to see how you two look in real life. I get the feeling you're an adorable couple."

"We're not a couple," Eiji said firmly. "Anyway, what is this man's second problem?"

"His second problem is that he is stubborn and refused to give in to suggestions from others." The old woman chipped a rough mortar shape free from the rest of the chunk of wood and began to refine it. "We all do to an extent. No one really likes to be told what to do but when you live that attitude to the fullest, you get our neighbour. His wife left him years ago because all he thought about and talked about was money and he was never open to suggestions, of any kind. His children tried for years to speak with him but he always cuts their visits short. He isolated himself."

"I see," Eiji said.

They sat in silence as the old woman finished making the mortar. Once it was complete Sesshoshi ground some rice in it and it turned to gold. When Eiji tried the rice melted into fowl smelling berries. She threw the mortar into the fire. "Sorry for destroying all your hard work." Eiji watched the mortar burn.

"You are as kind as the last visitor I had," the old woman said. Eiji smiled. *She is happy that the old woman is pleased with her.* Sesshoshi smirked.

"I wish you could remember who it was," Eiji said.

"Alas, I don't."

"Must we wait until the dog tells me to spread the ashes to do so?" Sesshoshi asked.

"Good memory," Eiji said. "I'm not sure. Can you take a nap?" She smiled widely at him.

"I will try." Sesshoshi leaned back against the wall and closed his eyes. He meditated for an hour. Thoughts and images of Eiji floated through his mind. It gave him a chance to really study her. In his mind her hair was unbound, and moved around her like a storm. Her brown eyes were soulful, unlike those of female yōkai. Her body was slim and soft. She lacked the muscular definition that yōkai had, but he found liked that better. In his mind Eiji moved toward him. He reached out and held her cheek in his hand.

Sesshoshi knew he should not indulge in these feelings. It would not be fitting for a yōkai Lord to court a human peasant. But in this world he was free of those judgments and it allowed him to see Eiji as he truly wanted to. His father had told him yōkai must start to grow closer to humans. Sesshoshi doubted that this was exactly what his father had in mind and he did not think it would stop the prejudiced judgment and outrage that would follow should Sesshoshi actually pursue a relationship with Eiji but he was sure it would soften the blow.

He was getting ahead of himself. He was a master of self control. For now, Eiji was pleasant to look at and he would continue to enjoy the moments where he was able to touch her. In his meditative mind, her cheek felt warm against his hand, but it was not as good as the real thing. When had he started to feel this way about her? Was it the first time they met? Sesshoshi was not sure but he knew that day he had gone to fetch Lord Ko he had been looking for something to spark his interest and Eiji had done just that.

A bark interrupted his thoughts. Sesshoshi looked past Eiji and saw the dog behind her. It told him without speaking to take the ashes and spread them on the cherry trees at the edge of the village.

Sesshoshi opened his eyes once he knew their next course of action. "Lets go." Eiji bid the old woman farewell and apologized again for killing her dog and burning her mortar. Eiji bowed and followed after Sesshoshi. He led them to a grove of cherry trees. It was easy to find, the smell from the flower buds provided a clear trail. He sprinkled the ashes from the burnt mortar onto each tree.

The trees bloomed in seconds. Eiji gasped in delight at their beauty. Sesshoshi plucked a pink flower from a nearby branch and moved to place it behind Eiji's ear. She froze. Her eyes were fixed on his hand. Sesshoshi watched in amusement as she seemed to forget how to breathe. He gently placed the flower behind her ear. His claws grazed her skin as he retracted his hand, leaving a tingling sensation where they had touched. *She is not a toy*, he reminded himself. *But she is so responsive.* Sesshoshi could not help but tease her. He was use to the cold distance that came natural to female yōkai. Even Eiji's most filtered responses were greater than the most expressive female yōkai.

Eiji was lost for words. Sesshoshi enjoyed her stunned silence. They were interrupted by a Daimyo passing by. His kataginu covering his shoulders were light blue and his kimono was black. The Daimyo called compliments to Sesshoshi as he passed and stopped to give him gifts. Eiji took the rest of the ashes from the mortar and blew them towards the Daimyo. The ashes floated an impossible distance and landed in the young man's eyes.

"I hate being the bad guy," Eiji said.

"You cursed old man! Throw him in jail for this offence against me!" The Daimyo cried as he wiped his eyes.

The members of the Daimyo's entourage grabbed Eiji by the arms and hauled her off to the village prison. Sesshoshi followed them. He did not like watching the samurai man-handling Eiji. He refrained from pulling them off of her. She needed to be exiled in order for the story to be completed. The samurai tossed her into the village's pit. Eiji hit the ground hard. It was a long fall.

Eiji dusted off her close and looked up at him. She appeared unharmed, bruised at most. Good. "A little help?"

"Perhaps I should leave you down there."

"You won't," Eiji said. When he made no move to help her out. She squeaked "would you?"

Sesshoshi jumped down into the pit. He landed beside her. It smelled like death and decay. He hooked his arm around her waist. "Hold on." Eiji had just enough time to wrap her arms around his neck before he leaped out of the pit. When they landed, Sesshoshi released her and Eiji stepped away from him. He instantly missed the way her body fit against his.

They left the prison and walked into town. All the villagers glared directly at Eiji.

"Shun him!"

"He's done enough damage here!"

Eiji looked from one angry face to the next. "I think I'm being exiled."

"It would appear so," Sesshoshi said. "This is the end of the story correct?" Eiji nodded. "Then let us find the exit."

"Your way out is in the forest. By the tree where you buried my dog," the old woman called from her front step.

"Thank you!" Eiji called back and bowed. Sesshoshi and Eiji walked directly to the woods. The voices of the irate villagers faded into the background. When they reached the stump where the tree had been, there was now a portal, just as when they left Momotaro's story.

They stepped into the white void of the Overworld. Eiji grew apprehensive beside him. Her eyes darted all around, looking for something. *She must be thinking about the unfinished works,* Lord Sesshoshi thought.

"We need to find The Tale of the Bamboo Cutter next," Eiji said.

There was a door to their right. Sesshoshi looked for other options but he found none. It seemed this transition would be a simple one. They reached the door quickly. Eiji nearly ran to it. It was clear that she wanted to leave the Overworld as fast as possible. He heard her sigh with relief when she read the kanji on the door. He looked at its title and found The Tale of the Bamboo Cutter. Sesshoshi opened the door and leaped inside, pulling Eiji behind him.

Chapter 9

Once again Eiji didn't know where they were. In Momotaro the story began with a boy inside a peach. In the Tale of the Bamboo Cutter a baby is found inside a bamboo stalk. In Momotaro, Eiji had found herself inside a peach pit, so she surmised that therefore they must be inside bamboo stalk now. She couldn't see a thing. She felt around and her hands quickly found smooth hard walls. Eiji slid down to a sitting position. As soon as she slumped back against the wall a wave of exhaustion crashed over her.

"I think we're inside a bamboo stalk. We have to wait to be cut out," Eiji said.

"I could cut us out."

"You could, but I need to rest my eyes. Let's wait until the story begins on its own," Eiji said as her eyes drifted closed. She was out in a matter of seconds, before Lord Sesshoshi could say anything to stop her.

Eiji woke to rhythmic banging.

She startled awake, trying to make out what was happening in the darkness. "Sesshoshi?" Eiji said, feeling around on the ground. She touched the tip of his toes and withdrew her hand quickly.

"Hn?"

"What's happening?" Eiji asked. The banging continued. She realized she hadn't called him _Lord_ Sesshoshi. She waited for him to notice. He either didn't or didn't feel the need to correct her.

"I do not know this story. Perhaps we are about to be cut out, as you said earlier," he replied. Eiji frowned at him in the darkness.

"In the Tale of the Bamboo Cutter, a childless elderly couple find a baby inside a stalk of bamboo."

"I am beginning to notice a theme in these fairytales."

Eiji laughed. "You're right. In this story, the baby is a

princess. She's very beautiful and five princes come to ask for her hand in marriage but she doesn't want to get married at all, so she sends them off to find ridiculous and impossible treasures. They all fail, but then the emperor takes an interest in her. She wants to get away from him and she cries at the moon, asking to be taken home. The story ends with the princess returning to live in her kingdom on the moon."

"I see," Lord Sesshoshi said. "So this banging is probably the old man chopping down the bamboo stalk."

"I guess so." Before Eiji could say anything further, the eerie green hue of Lord Sesshoshi's yōkai aura filled their surroundings and the walls around them fell away. Eiji squinted against the light. Lord Sesshoshi wrapped an arm around her waist and leaped through the jagged hole in the stalk. They landed on the ground in front of an old man holding an axe mid-swing. Lord Sesshoshi let go of her waist and Eiji stumbled forward. Just as in Momotaro, once they were free of their confines, they grew to their full size.

The old man stared at them. A bewildered look was etched into his wrinkles. "A baby inside the bamboo? How remarkable." When the old man spoke he looked directly at Sesshoshi.

Eiji watched that deadly glare form on Sesshoshi's face.

"He's not a baby. He's a yōkai lord," Eiji said. The old man didn't flinch, he continued to look at Lord Sesshoshi as if Eiji had never spoken. "Looks like I'm the invisible one in this story. Which means you're the princess." Eiji covered her mouth to keep from laughing. "You're going to be so beautiful."

Lord Sesshoshi glanced at her. "How amusing." He then looked at the old man. "Old man, we are visitors to your world. We must complete your story in order to move on to the next and return home. I am not the princess you always encounter."

"You sure are talkative for a baby," the old man said, his belly shook with laughter. "A visitor you say. We haven't had a visitor in years. I understand, Mama and I will let you move through the story as you need. Though I am sad I must wait to have my dear Kaguya-hime again – the real one, I mean." The old man rambled and Eiji watched Sesshoshi's claws flex and relax.

"We would like to get through this story as fast as possible," Sesshoshi interrupted. The old man stopped speaking.

"Right. Well this isn't a story that can be rushed. This is a story that takes time," the old man said. Eiji watched the corners of Sesshoshi's mouth curl down and she found herself frowning as well. They had been making such good progress.

"Ask him how long we must wait until the princes show up," Eiji said. Sesshoshi repeated the question.

"Oh, only a few days when we're on visitor time. When I have my darling Kaguya-hime here we get to spend sixteen long years with her before the princes show up," the old man said. "I'm called Taketori no Okina. Come with me. I'll show you to our home."

They followed Taketori no Okina through the thick bamboo forest and down a gentle slope. At the bottom of the hill was a hut with a straw roof. Inside an old woman sat weaving bamboo baskets. Eiji started to suspect that there was not much else to do if you found yourself an old childless woman in a fairytale.

The old woman looked up. "Our Kaguya-hime has returned." Her face broke into a huge smile.

"Not this time. We have a guest. A visitor to our world," Taketori no Okina said.

The woman gasped almost silently. "I see. How exciting. You may call me Mama-san. Make yourself at home until the princes come."

Sesshoshi gave them a slight bow. Eiji raised a brow — was he taking a liking to the old couple?

"Ask them if there's a stream near by. Then I can bathe," Eiji said.

"I am not yours to command," Sesshoshi said.

"No, but you need to be my voice. It's not my fault that they can't hear me," Eiji said, placing her hands on her hips. Sesshoshi repeated the question to the old couple. They pointed them to the north of where they had emerged from the bamboo forest. "There's a stream not far from here."

Eiji left the hut and headed for the stream. Sesshoshi was following her.

"Uh, you aren't planning on watching me bathe are you?"

"Why would I want to gaze upon a human body."

The comment hurt but Eiji pretended it didn't. "I didn't say you wanted to. So then *why* are you following me?"

"There is nothing else to do."

Eiji rolled her eyes. The sight of the stream put a smile on her face. The sun sparkled off the gently flowing water. It smelled fresh.

She glanced at Sesshoshi. "Uh..."

He turned his back. "I will not look."

Eiji didn't feel completely comfortable but the water was too inviting for her to deny herself a bath, peeping yōkai lord or not. Eiji removed her priestess garb and skipped towards the shore. A shiver ran up her whole body when her feet met the water. She missed the bath house at home but cold water was better than no water so she launched herself forward. Eiji scrubbed her skin and her hair. It felt wonderful to get the grime off her body.

Once she was satisfied, she exited the water and sat down on a rock with her back to Sesshoshi. She wrung out her long black hair. "I need to wait for the sun to dry me a bit before I get dressed. You can go do something else if you like."

"I know."

As Eiji dried in the sun, she thought of her father and Haruka. She wondered once again how her father was coping with her disappearance. He had already lost her mother, her grandmother and now Eiji was gone as well. *Not for much longer. I'll be back as fast as I can,* Eiji thought. She missed her late night baths with Haruka. Eiji wondered if Haruka had any new gossip to tell her or if Katsu had made any moves yet. Eiji looked over her shoulder. Lord Sesshoshi's back was still turned to her. "What's the deal with yōkai and half-yōkai?" Eiji asked.

Sesshoshi shifted a bit at her question. "We see them as a disgrace, as a representation of a yōkai that was weak willed and a human that was naive."

"Sometimes yōkai and humans love each other," Eiji said. When Sesshoshi huffed Eiji persisted. "Haruka's parents loved each other."

"Your half-breed friend?"

"Yes. Haruka's mother died protecting her village when Haruka was six. Her father loved her mother from the beginning until the day she was killed."

"Yōkai do not kill inter-species couples or their half-breed children, but humans do." Sesshoshi hadn't commented on Eiji's claim.

"But considering them vermin is so much kinder?" Eiji bit out. She was dry now. She stood and began to dress. She secured her hakama around her waist. "What do you have against humans anyway? You constantly insult my kind."

He was silent for a long while. Eiji finished dressing and turned to face him. Sesshoshi still had his back to her. He stood and turned as well, meeting her eyes. "Watching my father try to negotiate with the Shogun, the Emperor and his people has become tiring. Humans feel as if they are entitled to this world. They refuse to share, just like children. Humans kill yōkai. Sometimes with reason but mostly out of fear. It is weakness to be so controlled by one's emotions." His eyes grew hard as he spoke. Eiji didn't think anyone would be strong enough to bring down a yōkai of Sesshoshi's calibre but by the look on his face she must be mistaken. "Humans are too loving, too trusting, too emotional."

"Those sound like good things to me," Eiji said with a small smile on her face.

Sesshoshi chuckled. "You would think so."

Something about this tone made Eiji think he was insulting her. "What do you mean by that?"

"You are entirely too loving, too trusting and too emotional. You have fallen in love with every old childless couple we have met. You even cared for the old woman that hated you for looking like her neighbour."

Eiji opened her mouth to try and object but she realized quickly that he was right and laughed at herself instead. "But isn't it wonderful? How can you go through this world, a fairytale world, a world filled with creations, and not love the people you meet or the things you see?" Eiji folded her arms over her chest.

Sesshoshi only chuckled again. He looked at her as if she

were an adorable child which made Eiji annoyed. "I suppose I should be grateful for the ease at which you love. You love Lord Ko and I know he is happy for it," Sesshoshi said.

Eiji sighed. "I miss him."

"I know. And for those emotions my family is very grateful."

Eiji gave him a puzzled look.

"Lord Ko hates living at the palace. The day you found him and brought him back to us, he had masked his scent and run away. I knew he did not want any of us to find him. My mother was beside herself. I have never seen her in such distress." *So yōkai do care, at least about their children,* Eiji thought. "When Lord Ko returned he was different. The day he spent with you changed his mood. So we let him return to you and ever since he has been a happier child."

Eiji smiled brightly. "I'm glad. He's wonderful." Sesshoshi seemed to be watching her face very carefully. Eiji looked away from his gaze.

"I worry that Lord Ko will grow up and fall in love with a human."

The smile dropped off Eiji's face. "I highly doubt my influence will lead him down that path. I'm a mentor for him. But if he did, would that really be so bad?"

Lord Sesshoshi was silent for a moment.

"No."

She was surprised by his answer. She felt they had crossed a line. This conversation was not one typically had between a lord and one of his subjects. Sesshoshi was being personal with her. Eiji didn't want to push her luck further by asking him more questions, she wanted their conversation to end on a pleasant note. She started to walk back to the hut, not paying any mind to whether or not Sesshoshi followed her. He didn't. In fact he stayed away from the hut for most of the day. Eiji ate with Taketori no Okina and Mama-san. They were a delightful couple and Eiji enjoyed listening to their banter. It was difficult to be unable to converse but Eiji made the best of it.

Sesshoshi returned in the evening. He slept outside while Eiji slept on a futon in the corner of Taketori no Okina's hut. They didn't say a word to one another.

Chapter 10

Sesshoshi was growing restless. "How many days must we wait for the princes to show?"

"I don't know," Eiji said. He knew she did not know but she was the only one he could ask so he asked her a lot and she grew more and more annoyed each time. When he had asked Taketori no Okina earlier that day, he only repeated that they would come in *a few* days. This did nothing to settle him.

"Are we expected to sit around and wait?" He was pacing now.

Eiji rolled her eyes at him. "No one expects anything of us Sesshoshi. We're stuck in a fairytale world with only *one* quick route out. We have to get through this story or else we don't leave it. The princes will come when they come." Eiji had taken to the habit of saying his name without his title. He should correct her but he never did.

Sesshoshi stopped pacing and turned to her. "Let us train."

"Train?"

He enjoyed the surprised look on her face. "Yes train. To pass the time I will teach you how to fight."

Eiji's mouth dropped open. "Fight? I know how to fight... Sort of." He thought of her battle with the worm yōkai. She could use her scythe and reiki well enough but she was not masterful. He told her so and she huffed at him.

"As Lord Ko's mentor and protector you should master your weapon." Sesshoshi said. Eiji folded her arms over her chest. He could help her refine her skills and since she was not totally incompetent perhaps she would even provide him with enough of the challenge in combat to sate his boredom.

"I have no desire to be beaten into the ground by a yōkai lord. You're much stronger than me. It wouldn't be a fair fight anyway."

88

"You can use your reiki. But first we will work on your technique only." Sesshoshi could practically watch the excuses and arguments running about in her head as they passed through her brown eyes.

Finally she sighed. "Fine."

Sesshoshi turned and headed into the forest. Eiji followed and they walked until he stopped at a clearing.

"This will suffice." Sesshoshi turned to her. He grabbed her wrist and pulled her forward. Eiji stumbled into his embrace, face reddening every second.

"What are you doing?" She growled. "What has gotten into you."

That made Sesshoshi pause.

He was acting strange. He was bored beyond belief and the more they sat around the more he watched Eiji. And the more he watched her the more a feeling of attraction started to grow and he did not want to let that continue. He supposed that training her would only increase the time they spent together but he needed something else to focus on besides her pretty face.

"I do not know. All I know is I need a distraction. Now place your feet like this. This is zenkutsu."

Sesshoshi used his foot to shove Eiji's feet into the correct position – legs apart with one foot out to the left and one back. His hand felt warm as he placed it on her shoulder to angle her body better. He was touching her again. It was necessary to show her proper form. That was what he told himself, anyway.

"Now follow my movements. We will call these our mantras." He stood next to her in the same stance and started to slowly go through each different movement. Eiji blinked and then jumped into action. Sesshoshi nodded in approval as she tried her best to follow his motions, turning her wrists gracefully, moving her feet into the right positions.

They repeated the exercises for hours until he knew Eiji was exhausted. Her skin glowed with sweat and her eyelids were half closed. It reminded him of things he should not be thinking about.

"Not bad for a beginner," Sesshoshi said and straightened, moving out of the training stance. Eiji relaxed. Her legs collapsed under her and she sunk to the ground.

"Are you trying to kill me?" Eiji panted. She tried to steady herself with her arms but they wobbled like new bamboo.

"You kept up well," Sesshoshi said. Eiji looked at him as if he had grown two heads. "We will do a brief lesson on blocking a sword attack and then call it a day."

"More training? No, no, no, no." Eiji kept repeating but Sesshoshi was already pulling her up to stand once again.

Eiji's arms shook but she unhooked her scythe from her belt. *She is determined not to look weak in front of me,* Sesshoshi thought. Sesshoshi was true to his word. He instructed her how to throw her scythe to deflect a sword and then he let her rest.

"I'm going to go soak in the river," Eiji said, dragging her sore body down the hill and away from her merciless teacher. Sesshoshi took to widening their training clearing by cutting down bamboo with his claws. It felt good to destroy something and it kept his mind off of Eiji in the river.

The next day, Sesshoshi felt less restless but that did not mean he had given up on the idea of training. Eiji dragged herself after him as she followed him back to their training clearing in the woods. He could hear her feet scraping against the ground. It was obvious she was sore from the previous day. She walked stiffly, but she never complained. Sesshoshi worked with Eiji on the same training poses and movements she had done the day before. At the end of the day he introduced her to techniques with her scythe.

"How do you know how to use my weapon so well. I thought you only used your sword or your claws," Eiji asked. Sesshoshi moved to strike her with his sword and Eiji swung her chain upwards, deflecting the sword with her scythe.

"I have trained with all manner of weapons. The sword is simply the one I am best at."

"Oh. I see."

The days that followed were the same. Sesshoshi trained Eiji to alleviate his boredom and Eiji improved. Everyday before they trained, Sesshoshi caught Eiji glancing down the dusty path leading to the hut in hopes to see the princes approaching. Days had gone by and they had not come. At first Sesshoshi would look with her but now he found himself less eager for them to arrive. Once the story progressed it would mean they could move on and be closer to leaving this world but that would mean they would be back home, where humans and yōkai did not get along, where his time with Eiji would come to an end.

Eiji looked away from the path and followed after Sesshoshi. She gathered up her scythe as soon as she entered the clearing. Sesshoshi did not like to waste time. As soon as she turned, feet in the proper position, Sesshoshi was poised at the opposite end of the clearing.

"What lesson will you teach me today oh great Lord Sesshoshi," Eiji said and gave him a mocking bow.

"Today we will work on breaking away from an attack," Sesshoshi said. "And your attitude." Eiji laughed.

Sesshoshi lunged forward. He was in front of her in an instant. Eiji raised her scythe in front of her chest to block in a jerky, reflexive motion. She had nearly dropped it. Sesshoshi's sword collided with her scythe.

"That was pretty terrible Sensei," Eiji said. "I can't dodge or block yōkai attacks."

"I am well aware of that. Nothing wrong with a little fun during training. And your reaction would have spared your life, for a few moments anyway."

Eiji gave him an annoyed look. She pushed against his sword as he pushed against her scythe, neither of them making any moves away from each other.

"Are you going to make a move?" Eiji asked.

"That is your lesson for today," Sesshoshi said. "How to get out of this kind of situation and emerge with the upper hand."

"Ah." Eiji gave a slow nod of understanding.

"The fear here is that moving away from your opponent will allow them to strike you. You want to guide your opponent away from you so that you remain in control of the motion of the battle." Sesshoshi showed her how to angle her scythe so that his sword would slide up and away from her simply using the force he was using to push against her.

They practised this until Sesshoshi was pleased with her progress.

"Better," he said as his sword collided with her scythe once again.

Eiji was about to tilt her scythe and try the technique again when a voice shouting "Kaguya-hime! Kaguya-hime!" startled her. Sesshoshi felt her relax but he was still pushing against her scythe. The force sent Eiji falling backwards. Sesshoshi's arm shot out and he grabbed her around the waist, pulling her to him in an embrace that reminded him too much of lovers. Like opening the flood gates, his mind rushed with thoughts he had long been trying to hold back, the warmth of her body, the way his hand felt on her back, the way she stared at him with her lips parted slightly. He noticed these things when he had held her before, jumping out of the pit in Hanasaka Jii-san and leaping out of the bamboo days earlier. Sesshoshi had tried his best not to let his mind focus on those feelings then but his resolve had broken.

"Kaguya-hime!" Taketori no Okina's third yell sent Eiji back peddling away from Sesshoshi and Sesshoshi turned towards the old man.

"What is it?"

"The princes are here," Taketori no Okina said. He bent over and put his hands on his knees, breathing heavily.

"Thank you," Sesshoshi said. Eiji reluctantly put away her scythe and Sesshoshi slowly sheathed his sword. They returned to the hut at a leisurely pace.

Five princes sat on their knees on the ground in front of the porch. Sesshoshi stood before them. They all bowed low to the ground. Sesshoshi straightened a bit. He heard Eiji laugh quietly. He looked at her. Her eyes sparkled, clearly asking him *'Did you miss this kind of treatment?'*

The princes began speaking at once.

"Oh princess of flexible bamboos scattering light!"

"You are as beautiful as they say."

"I have come to ask for your hand in marriage."

"Wait a minute, that's why I'm here."

"Me too!"

"Me as well. How dare you interfere."

Eiji laughed. "Oh beautiful Lord Sesshoshi. Marry one of

them, oh please." She covered her mouth but couldn't stop giggling.

Sesshoshi looked over at her and she tried harder to stifle her laughter, shoulders shaking with effort.

"Princess what do you look at so fondly? Oh that you would gaze upon me in that way," one of the princes said.

"Remind me what I am required to do," Sesshoshi said.

"Right!" Eiji said. "You need to give them five impossible tasks. I'll tell you as you go along. First tell them you'll marry the first one that completes the task."

Sesshoshi did just that and with Eiji's guidance he told the princes what to do.

"You," Sesshoshi gestured to the first prince, "must get me Buddha's stone begging bowl. And you must get me the jewelled branch from Horai. From you I would like a robe made of fire rat hair. You must bring me a coloured jewel from a dragon's neck. And you must bring me a cowry shell born of swallows."

"Yes princess!" The princes shouted in unison. They scrambled to stand, pushing and shoving one another out of the way as they retreated back down the dusty path.

Sesshoshi looked at Eiji expectantly.

She smiled. "Now we wait."

Chapter 11

Eiji found herself in a rather interesting situation. She lay on her back, Sesshoshi above her, their lips were inches apart. His white hair fell over his shoulders, surrounding her. His breathing was quick and uneven.

"Lord Sesshoshi, what are you doing?" Eiji asked. She couldn't remember how they had gotten here. All she knew is that she really wanted him to kiss her. He said nothing, only growling in a low tone. *Possessiveness,* Eiji thought.

He closed the gap between them.

Their lips collided.

Eiji gasped with pleasure. His lips were soft and warm. She wove her fingers into his hair. Sesshoshi moved his hand to grip her side. His clawed fingers sliding down her waist in a way that made her whole body shiver.

He was about to move his warm fingers inside the lapel of her kimono when Eiji woke up. She sat up with a gasp, panting and flushed.

A dream.

It had been a dream.

Of course it was only a dream, Eiji thought once she had caught her breath. She put her hand on her racing heart. It would only ever *be* a dream. She needed to remember that. Eiji got up and went outside for some fresh air. Her mind replayed the dream over and over again even though she told it to stop. *This is going to be a long day,* Eiji sighed.

For today's training Sesshoshi had suggested they relax by grappling. *Great,* Eiji thought. *Just what I need. Contact.* When they trained with her scythe there was distance between them. Grappling would mean touching. Why did he have to suggest this today, of all days. She wanted to be far from him, to get her mind off her dream. As soon as she had seen him that morning, her pulse had sped up. The way he had kissed her in her dream played over and over again in her mind.

Eiji needed to focus. He was saying something. *Don't stare at his lips.*

"We will spar, just as you would fight with someone for fun," he said.

"I don't fight *for fun,*" Eiji said.

"Then today will be your first time." Sesshoshi circled her in the clearing and Eiji grew nervous. Her mind was distracting her. He pounced and Eiji barely had time to block before she stumbled backwards. He reached for her and Eiji put her hands out, allowing him to grab hold of her fists. It was a clumsy exchange.

"You're not trying very hard," Sesshoshi said. He was trying to move around her in ways that would make her react defensively but Eiji only swatted at him.

"I don't know how to fight like this," she said. *And your jawline is interfering with my ability to think straight.*

"Everyone can fight like this. Every species is born to defend themselves. Even young raccoon dogs know how to grapple," Sesshoshi said.

He swiped at her and Eiji ducked.

"At least you are moving now." Sesshoshi lunged at her again and she dodged. "Fight back."

"I –" Eiji felt her blood boil. She didn't like being toyed with. "I don't feel like it today.

"You're lying."

Eiji growled. "Don't read my feelings right now. I'm entitled to those in private. I'll share what I wish."

"Should I command you to as your Lord?"

"How dare you." She lunged at him and tackled him to the ground. She pushed reiki into her palms so it would hurt him. She managed to land a couple of punches before Sesshoshi regained his senses and took control. He pushed her off him and threw her onto her back. He pushed her down and held her arms above her head, using his legs to stop her from kicking him.

"There you go. Now you are fighting back," Sesshoshi hissed. This was too much like her dream. His face was so close to hers. Eiji had never been good at holding back her feelings. She didn't want to feel any sort of attraction to Sesshoshi but she'd be lying to herself if she said there was nothing there and she'd promised herself she'd stop doing that. There was *a lot* there. She knew he would never return her feelings and it killed her that some days she thought he might.

"You are still distracted." Sesshoshi pulled her up and into his lap. She pushed against his chest but he grabbed her wrists. Holding both of them with one of his hands, he grabbed her chin and guided her to face him. "You usually have an easy time telling me exactly how you feel. What is on your mind?" Sesshoshi said. His tone surprised her. He sounded like he cared. This made Eiji more irritated. She was a human and he was yōkai. Their worlds didn't mix well and he had, on more than one occasion, let her know that he wasn't fond of humans. But he sounded like he was interested in her feelings.

"It's complicated. I don't know if I'm ready to talk to you about it yet," Eiji said.

Sesshoshi released her chin. He let her slide off his lap and helped her stand. "Understood. Let us call it a day." He disappeared into the forest and Eiji went to the river to bathe.

Once she was in the water, Eiji swiped at the river like it had wronged her. A tight knot formed in her chest as the tension in her body grew. He infuriated her. Lord or not, she couldn't think it reasonable to demand to know her feelings. It was bad enough he could sense so much of them to begin with. Why had she fallen for him? *Am I destined to be old and childless, like all the elderly people we've met so far, but just not a couple?* Eiji growled to herself. She couldn't believe she had let herself grow fond of a yōkai lord. He would never love her in return. His pride, their species, his family would always separate them.

You're making a lot of assumptions on his behalf, Eiji thought. She silenced her mind. It was hoping, grasping at anything that would make her feel less like a fool.

She emerged from the river and dressed once the sun dried her body. She returned to the hut and settled down on her futon. The elderly pair couldn't see or hear her so she couldn't converse with them. Sesshoshi was nowhere to be seen and she didn't want to talk to him anyway. *Where is Haruka when you need her,* Eiji thought. What would her half-yōkai friend say? Eiji smirked. Haruka would say "Are you stupid? How can you be around Lord Sesshoshi all the time and not even *try* and put the moves on him."

Then Eiji would say. "I don't have a death wish."

"He can't kill you in this world. If I had the literal embodiment of a drool-worthy male specimen around me all the time I would try every trick I have."

"You *have* tricks. I don't."

"Eiji don't be so ridiculous. This is so typical of you. You don't see the way the men in the village look at you. All you need to do is smile and you'll have Regent Death himself at your feet."

"Haruka -"

"Don't *Haruka* me. We've had this conversation a million times. You need to do this for yourself. You can't keep denying yourself the basic pleasures of life. Just because you feel bad about your father being alone without your mother doesn't mean you have to be alone forever to make up for it."

Haruka was no help. Eiji closed her eyes. It didn't take long for her to fall into a dreamless sleep.

The next day, one of the princes returned. Eiji was surprised to see him back so soon. She turned to head to the forest to locate Sesshoshi but found him standing behind her.

Eiji jumped. "You startled me."

"Hn."

"One of the princes has returned," Eiji said.

"I can see that." Sesshoshi looked past her at the sweaty man trudging up the hill. "Which one is he."

"You asked him to bring you a coloured jewel from a dragon's neck." Eiji said. "He won't have it."

"I see," Sesshoshi said. He sat on the porch and waited for the prince to approach him.

"Kaguya-hime! I have returned from my dangerous journey," the prince said as he shuffled down the gravel path and fell to his knees before Sesshoshi.

"Do you have a coloured jewel from a dragon's neck?"

The prince looked at the ground. "No princess. I had to turn back because of a mighty storm. I was sailing across the vast ocean to reach the island where the dragon lay and a storm consumed our ship. I was awfully sea sick. We turned back, though I didn't want to. I hoped that my bravery would prove enough for you."

"No. You may leave," Sesshoshi said. He stood and headed back towards the forest.

Eiji followed after him. "Way to let a guy down gently." She could hear the prince wailing behind them, begging for Kaguya-hime to give him another chance.

"Why? Whether I say it gently or not is inconsequential as long as we advance the plot. He is not a real person anyway," Sesshoshi said.

Eiji doubted Sesshoshi would have been kinder if the prince was real. It pained her heart to hear someone so sad and she couldn't understand how Sesshoshi remained unaffected. Eiji wondered how Sesshoshi might handle her feelings if she was ever deeply upset.

"Come. We will train again today," he said. Eiji followed him to the clearing and picked up her scythe.

They spent the day training. She felt that Sesshoshi was no longer letting her win and that she posed a challenge to him at least a handful of the times they sparred. They didn't converse during their battles. It wasn't in her nature to be so quiet, but she found she kept her mind off of Sesshoshi better if she didn't have to listen to the sound of his voice.

Sesshoshi switched from sparring to their mantras. Eiji enjoyed how these motions were effortless to her now. She moved her arms and legs without thinking and enjoyed the flow of the different stances.

"Do you really think humans and yōkai will never have a better relationship," Eiji asked.

"Maybe one day."

"I see no reason why not."

"There are reasons that go back to the beginnings of time and that neither of our kind will ever forget," Sesshoshi said.

Eiji nodded. "I know. I just think that we can get past that." She wasn't sure if she was talking in the general sense or about the two of them.

"Of course you do."

Eiji smiled.

"Yōkai will need to bend and welcome humans soon."

"What do you mean?"

"Humans are building a weapon that will kill yōkai as easily as we can kill humans," Sesshoshi said.

Eiji stopped in the middle of the cat stance. "What?"

"Keep moving," Sesshoshi growled and Eiji resumed working through the poses. "It comes from the sailors that bring things from foreign lands. They must have better control of their yōkai populations where they are from."

"How terrible," Eiji said.

Sesshoshi raised a brow. "Terrible? I thought you might be pleased."

"I don't think forcing yōkai to treat us better because we can kill them is any way to build a relationship," Eiji said. She moved through her last pose and turned to face Sesshoshi. He finished his last pose as well. Eiji was struck once again by his grace. She loved watching the way he moved, how his hands swiped through the air, how his silver hair fell over his shoulders. She needed to stop thinking about it, she was starting to blush.

"You are staring," Sesshoshi said. Eiji flinched and moved her eyes from where they had been fixed on his chest to meet his gaze.

"I was not."

"Now you are lying."

"That is true," Eiji said. Sesshoshi took a couple steps towards her. She could feel the heat coming off his body. Eiji found it hard to breathe.

"Like what you see, priestess?" He said. Eiji looked away from him. He was toying with her. Sesshoshi placed a clawed finger under her chin and made her look at him.

"You are too easy to read. There are so many emotions that run across your face."

"How nice for you to be able to know exactly what's going through my mind but I have no clue what's going through yours," Eiji nearly hissed. He smiled, showing his sharp canine teeth. He was making it worse. Eiji let herself, for a moment, toy with the idea of kissing him. *Perhaps if I act on my urges they will go away,* Eiji mused. It made sense to her. She had never known the touch of a man and her body was going crazy at the slightest touch from Sesshoshi. If she let herself indulge in her fantasies perhaps her body would be satisfied and she could focus more on getting rid of her attraction to him. *But he would have to let you,* Eiji reminded herself. She knew he wouldn't. She was a source of amusement to him, that was clear, but nothing more.

"I am careful with the emotions I show on my face but I am not impossible to read. It is like fighting, you must know how to do it and know your opponent's weaknesses," Sesshoshi said. He brushed his thumb along her cheek.

"Let me guess. You have no weaknesses."

"Naturally."

"Ugh!" Eiji shoved him back but he didn't move. She only succeeded in pushing herself back a couple of steps but it was enough for her to feel like she could think again. Now that she was out of his grasp Eiji found it easy to be angry with him in order to rid herself of the longing she felt for him to touch her again. "You're so arrogant. Train by yourself today."

She turned and stomped out of the clearing. She expected Sesshoshi to stop her but he didn't. Eiji went back to the bamboo cutter's hut. She got there in time to see one of the princes coming up the dusty path. It was the one they had sent to retrieve the stone bowl of Buddha.

"Kaguya-hime! I have returned with the stone bowl of Buddha, just as you asked." The prince called as he approached the hut. *You're time to shine Lord Sesshoshi,* Eiji thought. She sat down on the front porch and waited.

She didn't have to wait long before Sesshoshi appeared. The exchange between the Lord and prince was quick and simple. The stone bowl didn't glow with holy light so Sesshoshi dropped it, destroying the bowl, and sent the prince on his way. Then he was gone again, leaving the prince to cry and pick up the pieces of the bowl. Eiji had to look away, she knew the princes were dishonest but she hated seeing anyone cry such sad tears. *Princess Kaguya must really be beautiful to evoke such a strong reaction,* Eiji thought. It was appropriate that Sesshoshi should fill her roll in this story. Eiji wondered what it would be like to be so beautiful that word of her beauty would spread all across Edo. She listened to the prince's sobs and decided it wouldn't be worth the attention.

Eiji looked out towards the horizon. The lake down the hill from the hut glimmered gently in the setting sun. *How far does this world go?* Eiji wondered. They had never been in a story long enough to slow down and think. This tale was progressing slowly. Perhaps she would have time to take a look around the land before the next prince arrived. Eiji retired for the night, determined to do some exploring the next day.

Chapter 12

Sesshoshi poked Eiji with his foot. It was time for them to train again. Though their last session had ended on a sour note he did not think that any reason not to continue with their lessons. Besides, he knew he had pushed her yesterday. It was mostly his fault. His senses told him that she desired him or at the very least she was attracted to him. He distracted her, enticed her and he watched her work so hard at keeping those feelings at bay. He did not want to admit to himself that he was doing the same.

Eiji grunted and rolled over. He nudged her again. "Wake up. Time for training." Eiji opened her eyes and seemed to notice him for the first time. She sat up quickly.

"Geez! You don't have to be so pushy. Or get so close." She scooted away from him.

"I did not know it bothered you so much." He did know. Eiji muttered something under her breath and then rose to get dressed. She was ready quickly. She stopped in the middle of securing her hakama around her waist and looked up at him as if she had remembered something.

"I was thinking that today we could explore the story world," Eiji said. "We don't know how far this area goes. It would be interesting to find out."

"Interesting?" He certainly would not call it that.

"I think so," Eiji huffed. It was so easy to get on her nerves. "I'll go by myself if you think it'd be boring. We can train after."

"I will join you," Sesshoshi said. He followed Eiji down the hill towards the lake. She turned to the east, towards a part of the forest that they trained in that ended near the edge of the lake. They walked for hours, finding nothing but wilderness and the occasional wild animal.

"What is it you are looking for exactly?" Sesshoshi asked.

"Nothing in particular," Eiji said. They were moving up a steep mountain side, the air was changing and Sesshoshi could tell they were nearly at the top. Eiji kicked a pebble with her toe.

She smiled guiltily at him. "Maybe I was hoping for a quicker exit. Perhaps the fairytale characters had failed to tell us about it. Or maybe they just don't know about any other route out of their world."

"I see."

"I also wanted a change of scenery," Eiji said. She reached a blockade of fallen logs and large rocks. Sesshoshi watched her climb over the pile. When she got to the top, she slid out of his sight with a yelp of surprise. He jumped over the pile in seconds and grabbed onto her. He had stopped her from falling off the sheer side of the mountain that was on the other side of the pile.

He pulled her to safety, holding on to her waist as they stood atop a large fallen log at the top of the pile. Eiji panted against his side.

"Sometimes I wonder if we could die here," she said in between breaths. "I know we can't kill each other but do you think this world could kill us?"

Sesshoshi glanced down at her, surprised.

"It could be possible." He looked down at the ground several ri below him. "We have determined we cannot hurt each other but that rule may not apply to our landscape."

"Or maybe the other characters in the stories. I wonder if they could hurt us," Eiji said.

"Hn." Sesshoshi hadn't considered it. It was rare that he ever considered the ability of something or someone to hurt him. Yōkai did not have to worry about that the same way that humans did.

"Uh, Sesshoshi?" Eiji said. "You can put me down now." He jumped back, off of the pile of broken trees, taking Eiji with him. He set her down and stepped away. They headed south until they came upon the clearing in the bamboo forest that they used for training.

"How strange. We were definitely heading south but this clearing is in the north," Eiji said. She came to a stop in the middle of the clearing.

"I will investigate." Sesshoshi took off in the direction

they had been walking. He retraced their steps, following Eiji's scent through the forest until he came upon her again. "It is a loop. Somewhere along the way it connects to itself."

"Makes sense, I suppose," Eiji said.

Sesshoshi raised a brow. "It does?" He wanted to hear her explanation.

"Sure. If we're trapped in a story that repeats itself over and over again then where else is there to go than back to the beginning."

Sesshoshi chuckled. He enjoyed the way Eiji's cheeks flushed when he laughed. "I suppose that does make sense." She smiled at him.

"I think I've had enough for today," Eiji said. "We can get back to training tomorrow."

Sesshoshi was pleased to find Eiji was up on time the next morning. They went to their clearing after their morning meal and started training immediately. Sesshoshi knew their warm up distracted her. She stole glances at him when she thought he was not looking.

He was always looking.

This morning, however, he found himself unable to focus as well. It was much easier to watch Eiji without being detected than it was for her to watch him. Sesshoshi observed the way her black hair fell over her shoulder when she twisted in a new direction, the way her eyes sparkled with determination.

She was chatty this morning. When they started sparring Eiji launched into all sorts of questions. Sesshoshi had yet to grow accustomed to someone who could talk so much. It was not unwelcome but his species was not very talkative and humans, at least this human, seemed to have no problem coming up with things to say.

"Do yōkai ever eat humans?" Eiji asked. He could tell she knew the answer already.

"Some do."

Her face looked exactly how he had expected it would.

"You knew the answer to that one."

Eiji sighed. "I suppose I did."

"You also know that yōkai that eat humans are regarded no more as a person as you would an oxen at the head of a plough. Higher yōkai such as myself do not eat humans."

"But you do kill them."

"Yes. I also kill my own kind if they deserve it. I have told you this before." Sesshoshi blocked her attack and side stepped her attempt to kick his feet out from under him. "You are upsetting yourself with your own questions. What is the point in asking them?"

"I don't know," Eiji said. She swiped at him again. They were both distracted and their sparring session lacked any real direction.

"That is something I find strange about you. You speak without implicit purpose," Sesshoshi said. That made her laugh. Eiji smiled brightly at him and he looked away.

"Why not? Words don't cost anything. You won't run out if you speak too much."

Eiji blocked his downward swipe.

"Words are powerful. If you chatter away people will view you as one without substance," Sesshoshi said. Eiji's face fell. She thought he had meant he thought she was without substance. He wanted to fix his mistake. "However, I can see with the way you use words more freely that there can be benefits without loss of dignity."

She smiled again. "I think that was a compliment. It was hard to tell." They took a break from training.

Eiji flexed and closed her hand a few times. "Ow." She whispered, rubbing her palm.

"What is the matter?"

"Hand cramp. My hand and wrist gets sore after a while."

"It takes a long time to build up stamina." He took her hand in his, enjoying the way her eyes widened at his touch. "I will show you a stretch." He held her arm out and faced her palm flat towards him. He pushed the tips of her fingers backwards until he heard her hiss.

"That hurts."

"It will feel better in time," he said. He kept her fingertips bent back slightly for a few moments longer. Sesshoshi turned her hand to lay within his and massaged her palm and wrist gently. Eiji's eyes started closing and she said nothing.

"If I knew it was this easy to subdue you, I would have done it sooner," Sesshoshi said. Eiji's eyes flew open and she glared at him. She tried to pull her hand back but he held it fast.

"Just relax," he chuckled. He massaged her hand a little while longer while Eiji looked at the ground beside her.

He wanted to touch her further. Sesshoshi was confident he knew how she would react. Eiji's body language was clear, she was attracted to him but he also knew she was trying to keep her feelings at bay. Would she reject him for this reason alone?

She puzzled him.

Yōkai females where easy to read. They hid their intentions better but they were clear and direct with their words. If Ritsuka was sitting in Eiji's position she would turn to him and say "I want to go to bed with you." There was no room for interpretation there, but Eiji wasn't like that and he was glad.

He moved his claws up her arm, massaging her forearm and pushing back the sleeve of her white hakui. Eiji's eyes widened but she didn't look at him. The blush on her cheeks was even more evident now.

He stopped massaging and simply let his hand drift along her skin. It was soft under his rough hands. He grabbed her arm and pulled her to him. Her gasp made him smirk. Eiji's breathing grew shallow as Sesshoshi snaked his arm around her waist. He ran his claws along the side of her face and pushed back her hair.

Eiji stared up at him with her mouth hanging open. He had never seen her so speechless before. He leaned down and captured her lips. Eiji was quick to respond, leaning in to the kiss. Sesshoshi pulled her tighter against him. He could feel both of their pent up frustrations coming out. He tangled his fingers in her hair as he ran his tongue along her bottom lip.

Eiji let out a deep moan that stirred something within him that had not been awake in a long, long time.

"Kaguya-hime! Kaguya-hime!"

Sesshoshi could have killed the old bamboo cutter. Eiji jumped away from him, leaving his body cold where she had been pressed against him. Sesshoshi watched her catch her breath and smooth out her hair.

"Kaguya-hime! More princes have arrived," Taketori no Okina said.

"Fine," Sesshoshi replied. The old bamboo cutter disappeared within the forest. Sesshoshi turned to Eiji. To his disappointment she looked like she did when she was trying to push down her feelings towards him.

"Sesshoshi, I –" Eiji began. He could tell he would not like where this was headed.

He grabbed her chin and kissed her again. "We will finish this later." He turned from her and headed back to the hut. He did not dare look at her but Eiji's energy remained the same. Perhaps his promise would convince her not to run from her feelings any longer.

Chapter 13

Eiji followed Sesshoshi back to the hut where the princes would be waiting. Her heart still pounded and she was still catching her breath. The kiss had been a shock but so had his gentle touches. Eiji wanted all of it again. There was a nagging voice at the back of her mind that warned her about getting emotionally attached to Sesshoshi. *Even if he likes you there will be no future for the two of you once you leave the fairytale world,* Eiji's mind lectured. She had initially tried to push her feelings away when Taketori no Okina had interrupted them but Sesshoshi's words to her had held a promise that his actions weren't solely impulsive. Besides, that voice nagging at her to stop was getting quieter. She was pretty sure her desires were stomping it out. Forcefully.

Apparently today was to be eventful. Eiji saw that two princes and one adviser awaited them at the hut. Sesshoshi sat down on a silk pillow before the three men, who bowed low to him. The princes clamoured for Princess Kaguya's attention, speaking over one another and shoving each other where they sat.

"Kaguya-hime I have brought you the robe of the fire rat."

"Kaguya-hime behold the jewelled branch from Horai."

Sesshoshi glanced at Eiji. "What now?"

"The robe of the fire rat will burn and the jewelled branch is fake," Eiji said. She watched as Sesshoshi took the fire rat robe inside and placed it in the fire that burned under a pot of bubbling grass tea in the earthen corner of the hut. The prince that had delivered the robe began to sweat and rightfully so since it didn't take long for the robe to catch fire. Hair of the fire rat was legend to be immune to any flame and therefore this robe was clearly a fake.

Next Sesshoshi flicked the jewels off the jewelled branch of Horai with his claws. The jewels should have been deeply embedded in the branch as the tree of Horai produced jewels as its fruit but this branch was fake.

"You have failed to bring me what I asked. Dismissed," Sesshoshi said. Eiji smirked, that was likely as theatrical as Sesshoshi would get when playing the part of a story character. The princes cried and wailed and left the way they had come, leaving just the adviser.

The adviser bowed low. "I have come to inform you that my prince lost his life in the pursuit of a cowry shell born of swallows."

Sesshoshi's eyes widened slightly. "Someone lost their life over this?" He was speaking to Eiji.

"Yes. It's a rather shocking part of the story. I remember the first time my grandmother read it to me it made me feel ill thinking that someone had died because Kaguya-hime ordered them to do impossible things. I imagine she felt the same way," Eiji said.

"Hn." Sesshoshi turned his attention back to the adviser. He bowed slightly. "I am sorry for your loss," he said nothing further and the man left.

Sesshoshi rose from the silk pillow. "What happens next?"

"Next the emperor Mikado will come and ask to marry you. He'll claim it was love at first sight. Then you must cry when the full moon comes out and your people, the people of the moon, will come and take you home," Eiji explained. The look on his face was comical and she smiled.

"The princess is from the moon?" Sesshoshi said.

"Yes. She was born there and sent to earth because she thought she would be happier here. When the pressure of marriage to a man she doesn't love proves too much she cries and wants to run away. Her people take that as a sign she's done with her time on earth and come and collect her," Eiji said.

"How ridiculous," Sesshoshi said. Eiji laughed.

The sun was going down and it was time to retire for the night. Eiji looked toward the hut where she usually slept alone. She started to walk toward it.

Sesshoshi grabbed her wrist and pulled her after him.

He led her back to their clearing.

"Is this where you've been sleeping?" Eiji asked.

"It is as good a place as any."

She didn't want to look at him. Now that the princes were gone and there were no more distractions for the rest of the evening, what would happen? *What do you think he'll do? Confess his love for you?* Eiji thought. *No, but he might touch you again.* She tried one last time to distance herself from her feelings but it was no longer working.

When she turned around she found him right in front of her. Eiji yelped in surprise.

She hit him in the chest. "I told you not to scare me like that!"

"You were quite lost in your thoughts," Sesshoshi said. Eiji shrugged but said nothing. She didn't think there was anything to add.

Sesshoshi placed his hands on her shoulders and ran his fingers down her arms. She tingled everywhere they touched. Her heart jumped to her throat. When his hands reached the end of their trail, Eiji grabbed his wrists. "What are you doing?"

It was a question, not an accusation.

"Did I not say we would finish where we left off?" Sesshoshi said. His golden eyes bore into hers. She could see affection in them and she hoped she wasn't wrong.

"You did."

Eiji let go of his wrist. He ran his fingers along the side of her neck and tangled them in her hair.

Eiji sighed and Sesshoshi stilled. "What happens when we leave this world? When we're back home where I'm a human and you are yōkai."

"You are a human now," Sesshoshi said.

Eiji rolled her eyes. "You know what I mean." His other hand found her waist and he pulled her to him.

"I have tried to deny myself these feelings I have for you. I do not wish to any longer. When we are back home I will not hide whatever we will become, but I cannot make promises of a future that I know nothing about," Sesshoshi said. She knew he would say something like that but she also knew he was right.

His hand moved up her side.

Would it be so bad to give in? Even if it was temporary,

would it be terrible to let herself have what she wanted?

Eiji decided it would be, as Sesshoshi might put it, not unwelcome.

She closed her eyes and stopped fighting. She heard the sound of him inhaling deeply as he took in her scent. He pulled her closer to him. Eiji felt small in his arms. It occurred to her that she was being held by one of the most powerful yōkai in the world, which only made her feel littler in his embrace.

She had yet to touch him. All this time she had been thinking of him and now he was hers to play with.

Eiji ran her hand along his bicep, enjoying the hard muscles that stiffened under her finger tips.

She looked into his eyes and saw the affection in them. His eyes moved to her lips. She gasped when his lips met hers. His kiss held all the affection she had seen in his eyes. Eiji was new at this but luckily Sesshoshi was patient and an easy lead to follow.

Sesshoshi pulled her to the forest floor. He slid his hand inside her hakui and pushed it from her shoulders. The feel of his skin on hers made Eiji suck in a breath. It made it more real for her. What were they doing? She found that she was sick of this part of her mind and as Sesshoshi ran his hands along her shoulders it was easy to ignore.

Sesshoshi removed his kimono and Eiji couldn't take her eyes off his chest. He chuckled at her expression.

She reached her hand out tentatively, wanting to touch him again.

He grabbed her hand and pulled her closer, placing her palm against his chest. Eiji glanced at him quickly for reassurance and then ran her hand along his skin. She buried her nose in his neck, inhaling deeply to take in the smell of him. He smelled like the forest in the morning. She kissed his neck and moved up to his jaw. He growled with contentment as she kissed along his jawline and found his lips once again.

Sesshoshi rid them both of their clothing. He pushed Eiji into the soft moss, moving over her in a possessive way that made her breath hitch.

She felt like prey.

She felt a pressure at her entrance and sucked in a breath. Sesshoshi kissed her cheek and then pushed inside her. Eiji gasped and arched her back. It was unlike anything else she had ever experienced, and she thought for a brief moment that Haruka had been right about the stupidity of denying herself these kinds of pleasures. He kissed her once more before he started moving. His pace was controlled and measured.

Eiji's heart fluttered when she heard rumbles of pleasure coming from him. Her head tilted back and her eyes closed as he quickened his pace. She ran her hands along his chest until they found his shoulders where she gripped tightly. Pressure started to build in her stomach. He moved faster. Eiji couldn't breathe when her body involuntarily convulsed. He followed shortly after, throbbing inside her. His movements stilled and he panted above her. Eiji met his gaze, his amber eyes stared deeply into hers. He disentangled himself from her and lay down in the moss next to her, pulling her close.

Eiji caught her breath and once her mind had caught up with her body she started to worry she had done it all wrong. What if he hadn't liked it?

"I –" Eiji began but Sesshoshi silenced her by rolling over and giving her a long, deep kiss. He pulled away from her and looked into her eyes.

"You know what I enjoy most about you?" Sesshoshi asked.

"No."

"Your responsiveness. Yōkai females do not make the faces you make, just now and in general, and they definitely do not make the noises you do," Sesshoshi growled. A hot heat filled her cheeks and also her belly. She was a little embarrassed by his words and his casual attitude towards what they had just done.

"We will make sure you get more practice," he said and lay down beside her once again. Eiji only nodded. She thought she would have trouble falling asleep, but with her heart and body satisfied sleep claimed her quickly.

She awoke the next morning still laying in Sesshoshi's arms. She closed her eyes and enjoyed the soft feel of his skin for a few moments longer before sitting up. She grabbed her clothing and ran naked down to the lake. There were certainly perks to being invisible within a story world especially now that the only yōkai who could see her had seen all of her.

Eiji bathed in the lake and emerged feeling powerful. As she lay in the sun to dry off she tried not to let her mind wonder back to the previous night. Sesshoshi's hands had been gentle and warm. She sighed to herself, and he was a really good kisser. Eiji dressed and when she turned back towards the hut she could see Sesshoshi coming down the hill towards her. He was in front of her in an instant.

"Good morning," he said and pulled her to him. Eiji wasn't accustomed to him being so open with his affection, in fact she wasn't use to him being affectionate at all. He nuzzled his nose into her hair. Eiji knew this was a yōkai thing. It allowed them to get the pure scent of their mates.

"Good morning," she said.

"The emperor is on his way," Sesshoshi said. Eiji nodded. She found herself reluctant to let the story progress. The sooner they made their way through the story, the sooner they would be back in their world and she wasn't sure what would happen to their relationship then. Sesshoshi stepped back from her and they returned to the bamboo cutter's hut.

"The emperor will be here any minute," Taketori no Okina said. No sooner had he said it when Emperor Mikado appeared over the hill and made his way to the front porch.

"Kaguya-hime! I have heard of your beauty from across the land," the Emperor began. It turned out that this was the beginning of a rather long speech about the Emperor's journey, his search for love, all the feelings he was feeling now that he lay eyes on the Princess Kaguya.

Eiji stood behind Sesshoshi and rested her hands on his shoulders. "You know, when I was a kid and my grandmother would read me this story I always thought I would want to be as beautiful as Kaguya-hime. I was in love with Emperor Mikado and I wanted him to be my husband," Eiji said quietly into his pointed ear.

"And what do you think of your husband now that you have met him in person?" Sesshoshi questioned with a smirk on his lips.

"I think I prefer yōkai lords," Eiji said. She heard the low rumble that emanated from Sesshoshi's chest and it made her smile. She spent the rest of the Emperor's speech playing idly with Sesshoshi's long white hair.

"And so I have come to you today to make you my wife," Emperor Mikado finally finished.

"I am guessing I have no choice," Sesshoshi said to Eiji.

The Emperor responded. "It is a great honour for a country girl to marry an emperor."

"Ooo, he sounds like you when you talk about the differences between humans and yōkai," Eiji said. Sesshoshi huffed.

"Do not do me any favours," Sesshoshi said to the emperor.

"You will be my bride! I will come for you tomorrow," Emperor Mikado said. He rose and left.

Eiji glanced up at the sky. "Now you have to cry at the moon. Can you even cry?"

"I am capable, yes, but I can not cry over nothing," Sesshoshi said.

"But you're suppose to be *so* sad about the pressures of marrying someone you don't love," Eiji said. Sesshoshi gave her a look that told her he was unaffected by this pressure. "You'll need to cry. We'll figure something out."

"We shall resume our training until this evening," Sesshoshi said. He turned on his heel with the expectation that Eiji would follow. She smirked in spite of herself. She'd follow him because she wanted to be close to him and she was sure he enjoyed knowing that.

They reached the clearing and started moving through the mantras. Eiji was usually distracted by Sesshoshi during this time but it was even worse now that she knew what lay beneath his robes. She was pleased to find Sesshoshi equally distracted. He was sneaking glances at her just as often as she was looking at him.

Once they were finished their warm up, Eiji grabbed her scythe. When Sesshoshi was ready, she attacked first. She met him in the middle of the clearing, swinging her scythe towards his chest. She infused the scythe with a bit of reiki to keep him on his toes. Sesshoshi blocked her easily and she pushed against him. They broke apart when Eiji side stepped him and pulled her scythe away without opening herself up to a blow.

Sesshoshi swiped low and Eiji blocked again. She was trying to figure out how to release her scythe without letting him land a blow on her shins and how to stop thinking about his hands on her, when his sword fell away. Eiji stumbled forward and into Sesshoshi's embrace.

He pulled her to him and captured her lips.

This time Eiji felt like she knew what to do. She tangled her hands in his hair, pulling him closer. He growled in approval. Her hakui fell away and she pushed his kimono off his shoulders. Once their clothing was gone, Eiji's hands found his chest. She moved them along his hard muscles and down his hips. She heard him gasp in pleasure and she smiled to herself. He pushed her against a nearby tree. The bark dug into her back but it was not unpleasant. He lifted her up and entered her. Eiji hissed with pleasure and grabbed his shoulders. When he began to move she could no longer think of anything else. Waves of pleasure washed over her with each thrust.

"Oh Sesshoshi."

He growled low in his throat and thrust faster and harder. Eiji rested her forehead on his and panted along with him. Her body tightened and shook when she hit her peak. In a couple of thrusts he was there with her. His movements stilled slowly and Eiji began to catch her breath. He slid out of her and placed her on the ground. Her legs were shaky.

"I need a bath," Eiji laughed. "Again."

"Hn." Sesshoshi picked Eiji up, grabbed their clothing and raced down to the river. Eiji shrieked as they moved at the speed Sesshoshi usually travelled. She couldn't see a thing, all the trees were a green streak until they were gone, replaced by the blue streak of the sky and river. Sesshoshi stopped before the river and dropped their clothing on the rocks. He dumped both of them into the river.

"Ah! So cold," Eiji said.

"I thought you would be use to it by now." Sesshoshi smirked at her shivering.

"I'm never use to that first dunk." Eiji's shoulder's shook but she soon grew accustomed to the water. Eiji scrubbed and washed her body. She helped Sesshoshi wash his long hair. Then she slid her hands over his shoulders and down his chest. He growled with pleasure.

"I don't want to leave this world," Eiji said quietly in his ear as she hung off his back. She felt him nod.

"Neither do I."

Eiji didn't want to think about how her relationship with Sesshoshi would look when they were back in their own world. She didn't want to have to live without his presence, without his touch. Once they were clean they lay on the rocky shore and dried off. Eiji closed her eyes and drifted off to sleep for a short while.

When she woke, Eiji sat up and dusted herself off. It was dark now and the moon was out. "Sesshoshi –"

"I know," he rumbled. He pulled her in for a kiss and then rose. They both dressed in silence.

Eiji looked at him expectantly. "Well? Cry."

Sesshoshi lifted her chin with his clawed finger. "Cheeky. We will need to come up with some other way." He released her and Eiji stepped back. She felt like they needed more distance between them if they were going to figure this out.

"What if you think of something sad," Eiji said.

"I do not get *sad* often," Sesshoshi said.

"Tears of happiness?" Eiji tried.

"No."

"Do you have any emotions at all?" Eiji said. She regretted her words instantly. "Sorry. I know you do."

"Hn."

"What if we just splash water on your face and you look at the moon?"

"That could work," Sesshoshi said. They walked down to the lake together. Eiji dipped her fingers in the water and sprinkled a few drops on Sesshoshi's cheeks. He looked up at the moon.

The clouds began to move away and the moon shone brighter.

"That'll do it," Eiji said. There was a tiny shape that appeared in the centre of the moon. Eiji squinted to see what it was. She didn't have to wait long before it grew closer. She could now make out the procession of moon people coming towards them. Eiji remembered that in this part of the story, the bamboo cutter or the emperor's guards would try and stop the princess from leaving, but the bamboo cutter must not have cared since his Princess Kaguya wasn't his real daughter and the emperor had left no guards.

The moon people rode in on a cloud that swept them across the sky like a magical tatami mat. They landed in front of Sesshoshi. Eiji could see they had abnormally large eyes. They reminded her of a preying mantis. Their foreheads were adorned with jewels and their robes were made from the finest silk.

"We have come to bring you home princess," a man said. He was the tallest and most elegant of them all. Eiji surmised he must be Kaguya's true father.

"Let's go," Sesshoshi said. The man and the rest of the moon people looked at him in surprise. Eiji smiled. Kaguya must fight being taken away from her earthly home every time. Eiji found that odd considering Kaguya would return to her birth place within the bamboo at the end of every story cycle.

That's when Eiji remembered.

There was a robe.

A feather robe of the moon that made Kaguya forget her time on earth. Perhaps it worked too well and at the beginning of each story cycle it made her forget the moon people entirely and when they came for her it really was as if she was leaving for the first time. *It would be awful to relive that over and over again,* Eiji thought. *I wonder if that robe could make me forget Sesshoshi.*

"I am not your princess. I am a guest," Sesshoshi said.

The moon people looked at one another. Kaguya's father nodded. "I see. We will see her again next time. I assume you seek the exit."

"We do," Sesshoshi said.

Eiji remembered another part of the story. "Sesshoshi, we're suppose to give the bamboo cutter the elixir of life and your robe. Well Kaguya's robe which you never wore. I think we can forget that part."

Sesshoshi nodded at her. "Where is the elixir of life?" Sesshoshi asked the moon people. Kaguya's father handed it to him. He placed it on the ground. "The old man will find it."

"I guess he will. He knows his own story well enough," Eiji said. Just like in the story of Momotaro where they hadn't escorted the treasure back to Momotaro's parents, Eiji hoped they would be able to bypass this detail as well.

Kaguya's father motioned them to follow. He led them through the entourage of moon people to the back of the cloud they travelled on. Eiji looked from face to face. Their skin was as smooth as porcelain and their hair long and flowing.

A bright red robe caught her eye. *That must be the feather robe,* Eiji thought. She walked over to it and touched its silky exterior. Eiji peeked inside one of the sleeves. The inner lining was like a dark void. It was no normal silk, it must have been woven out of magic. Eiji carefully tied the robe around her waist inside her own hakui. The moon people watched her but they didn't say or do anything. Eiji took that as permission enough.

Maybe it won't last once we leave this story, Eiji thought, but the dumpling from Momotaro had. There was only one way to know for sure.

"Eiji. Are you coming?" Sesshoshi said. The way he said her name sent shivers up her spine.

"Yes." She ran to catch up to him.

"What were you doing?"

"Just looking. I always thought the moon people would be beautiful but I didn't think they'd be this memorizing," she said.

"Hn."

Their exit was up ahead and together they left through the glowing door at the end of the tale of Princess Kaguya.

Chapter 14

Sesshoshi hated the white expanse of the Overworld. It made all of his senses go crazy. The sooner they got out of there the better. Eiji stood by his side looking smaller and more delicate than usual. *It must be this world. It looks like it will swallow her,* Sesshoshi thought.

"Where are we going next?" Sesshoshi asked.

"Kotutori jii-san," Eiji replied.

"We should get out of here as quickly as possible. There is a door over there," he said and pointed to the blue door off in the distance.

"You don't have to tell me twice," Eiji said. Together they moved towards the door, Eiji following slightly behind him.

A song floated by them.

Kagome, Kagome
The bird in the cage,
When, oh when will it come out

Sesshoshi noticed Eiji had stopped walking. He stopped as well. "That is the song you were singing with Ko." Eiji nodded, frozen with fright.

In the night of dawn
The crane and turtle slipped
Who is behind you now?

Eiji's eyes widened as if she knew exactly who was behind her.

A fear unlike any he'd ever felt before shot through him. An unfinished being that looked like the incomplete torso of a naked woman appeared behind Eiji. It moved like a song.

Sesshoshi raced toward her. Eiji caught his gaze just before the creature grabbed her and together they disappeared.

Sesshoshi reached for them but his claws swiped through nothing but air.

She was gone.

His chest felt tight and his breathing grew faster. He had never felt like this before. Yōkai were not safe from death, but he was not accustomed to having to worry about anyone's mortality. For the first time he did not know what to do. There had to be some way he could get to her. A place where unfinished beings go with their victims perhaps.

But where?

How would he find such a place? He looked from left to right and found nothing but blue doors floating around him. It would take him too long to search the Overworld for a place that might not even exist.

Sesshoshi turned around and froze when he saw a woman.

At first he thought she was another unfinished being but it did not take him long to realize that she was not. This woman was about the same height as Eiji, in fact she looked a lot like Eiji, only much older. Her hair was long and black, and she wore a green silk kimono.

"Who are you?" Sesshoshi asked.

"I am Tsuru," she said.

Sesshoshi remembered how fondly Eiji had spoke of her grandmother and how her grandmother had read fairytales to her when she was a child. Then he remembered how many times the characters of the stories they had travelled through mentioned a previous visitor, and that Eiji had told him her grandmother said she had been to the fairytale world before.

"You are Eiji's grandmother," he said.

"That was quick. Yes I am. How do you know her?" Tsuru asked. She folded her hands inside her kimono sleeves and waited patiently for his answer.

"We came to this world together through a scroll in your house," Sesshoshi said.

Tsuru clicked her tongue. "I told her not to touch that one."

"It was my fault," Sesshoshi admitted. There was no one else around except this old woman so he did not think it would do him any harm to admit fault.

Tsuru smiled warmly. "I know my Eiji. She would have found her way here with or without you."

"You are dead," Sesshoshi said.

"Oh I probably am. In your world, anyway," Tsuru said. Sesshoshi raised a brow.

"You see when I was young I came to this world on my own. I took the short cut through the stories the first time, just as you are doing now."

Sesshoshi was going to ask her how she knew that but the old woman just kept talking.

"I went through this world many times, exploring every story I could. When I knew I was getting too old for this, I wrote my own story and hid it somewhere no one should be able to find it. I made myself young, fast and strong – a walker of the fairytale world. I can find any story quickly and watch it unfold as an observer or enter it myself."

"So you are not Eiji's real grandmother. You are a fictional version of her that is optimized to function in this world," Sesshoshi said.

"Exactly."

"Eiji was taken by an unfinished being," Sesshoshi said. "Do you know how to get her back?"

"I've dealt with unfinished beings before but unfortunately there is nothing we can do for Eiji," Tsuru said. Sesshoshi felt his heart drop. "She will need to save herself by completing the project in some way. Then she will emerge from their world."

"So I must wait," Sesshoshi said. He was relieved to hear that Eiji was not lost to him forever but the prospect of standing around, waiting to see if she would survive her encounter did not sit well with him.

"You must wait." Tsuru nodded. "I'll make us some tea. I know my Eiji, she'll get through this." A gold door appeared before them and Tsuru opened it. She bowed to Sesshoshi and bid him to enter. Inside the door was a cozy room. It felt like a den, but of the human variety. Tsuru moved to the small fire in the unearthed centre of the room and started preparing some tea.

"She will be happy to see you when she returns,"

Sesshoshi said.

Tsuru stilled in her movements. "I won't be seeing her."

"Why not?"

"Eiji loves me and in her world I am dead. You know how real this world can feel. She will cling to me as if I'm the real thing. I know her heart. She mustn't see me or she will think she's abandoning her real grandmother but I am no more real than Momotaro," Tsuru said.

"She has loved every character she has met in this world." Sesshoshi nodded his understanding.   Tsuru laughed and shook her head. "That sounds like my granddaughter alright."

"She loves freely."

"Isn't it wonderful?" Tsuru smiled.

"It is – not unwelcome." Sesshoshi folded his legs beneath him and sat down. Then he waited.

Chapter 15

Eiji shoulders burned where the creature had grabbed her. She hadn't felt real pain in such a long time that she was stunned by it. The unfinished being let her go and Eiji stumbled back a few steps. They were in a dim room.

No, not a room.

It looked more like a hollowed out dirt cave. The ground beneath her feet was dusty and the walls crumbled around her.

The unfinished creature swayed before her. Its shape shifted from the naked torso of a woman to that of a man. It had no face and it moved in a rhythmic way that reminded Eiji of a song.

What was she going to do? If she could feel pain, like the way her shoulders burned, then she guessed that the creature could kill her. This wasn't a story or a game anymore. Eiji was fighting for her life and she had no clue how to do it.

She watched the being move for a while. It hovered before her in a silent threat to strike.

Then it started singing.

> Kagome, Kagome
> The bird in the cage,
> When, oh when will it come out
> In the night of dawn
> The crane and turtle slipped

The creature disappeared as it started its song. Eiji whirled around trying to locate it but she couldn't see it. It was as if she was alone in the dirt cave with nothing but the song floating around her.

"Who's behind you now?"

The singing stopped.

Eiji felt the creature to her left and she turned to face it. The unfinished being started to sing again. It sang the entire song and asked the question again.

"Who's behind you now?"

Eiji thought the being was to her right but she was wrong. The creature laughed and Eiji's hair stood on end. It appeared before her and swiped at her with long claws that hadn't been there before. Its hand became like a nata the villagers used to cut down crops back home and scratched Eiji across the chest. Her clothes protected her a bit but the claws still managed to rip through her kimono and rake across her skin. The wounds burned and stung and bled.

The creature began to sing again. It sang and sang and Eiji guessed and guessed where it was. When she was right nothing happened and when she was wrong it attacked her.

Her blood dripped onto the dirt floor of the cave.

Eiji's arms and chest were covered in wounds. *What do I do? How do I make it stop?* Eiji thought. She couldn't physically fight back. She tried to attack with her scythe and reiki but the creature was immune.

"Who's behind you now?"

Eiji was wrong again and when the creature appeared before her she tried again to use her reiki to purify it. The pink light that shone through her palms did nothing. The creature scratched her again, spilling more of her blood. This creature was not yōkai like the worm that attacked her village or Sesshoshi. Her reiki had no effect.

Eiji had always thought that the song sounded unfinished. Now she was certain she was right. *Maybe I have to finish it to defeat it,* Eiji thought. *I'm no lyricist. But maybe I don't have to be good to finish the song.*

"Who's behind you now?"

Eiji had always thought Kagome was a person though there were other interpretations of the song. Eiji decided to stick with that and test her theory.

Sesshoshi, Sesshoshi
Wolf in a cave
Backed by honour and doubt
Caught in the middle

Of a great divide
Who'll find you out?

The creature reeled back. Chunks of dirt flew up from the blood soaked ground around her feet and started to pack around the creature.

It kept singing but so did Eiji.

Eiji, Eiji
Girl in a dream
Crying at the corner of town
In twilight after dawn
Near the edge of the moon
Who'll defend you now?

The dirt continued to pack around the abomination. The more dirt that encased the unfinished being, the more Eiji was able to see a way out. She ran past the being. It swiped at her, drawing more blood from her arm as she sped past it.

Eiji headed where light began to appear at the back of the cave. The creature kept singing but its voice was muffled by the dirt that surrounded it.

Up ahead Eiji saw a golden door.

Relief flooded through her. *That must be the way out,* Eiji thought.

The creature's voice was growing louder. "Kagome, Kagome." Eiji listened to it sing the song. She glanced behind her and the creature was on her heels. Eiji's blood loss was starting to affect her ability to think. She could barely put one foot in front of another let alone think of another verse of the song. *I need to slow her down again. Think of something.*

Eiji ran.

"Eiji, Eiji. Not what it seems."

"The bird in the cage. When, oh when will it come out."

"Love, affection and drought. In the dragon's tear."

"In the night of dawn."

"The weak of heart reside."

"The crane and turtle slipped."

Eiji slammed into the golden door. She wretched it open.

"Who's your leader now?"

"Who's behind you now?"

Eiji tumbled through the door but not before the creature raked its claws along her back. She shrieked from the pain. Eiji twisted around as fast as she could, her back burning. She pushed the door shut with her feet, trapping the creature inside. She didn't know if the door would keep it inside. The creature had, after all, found her in the Overworld.

Eiji heart dropped as the unfinished being burst through the door, knocking Eiji back. Eiji pushed herself away as far as she could but her strength was gone. Her limbs shook and her vision blurred.

White fabric moved in front of her.

Sesshoshi. Eiji saw his white hair settle behind him as he came to a stop.

Eiji couldn't see what he did next but the creature was screaming. Then he scooped her up in his arms and took off in the opposite direction.

"It'll catch us," Eiji said, her voice shook.

"I can out run the unfinished creatures," Sesshoshi said. Eiji peeked over his shoulder. Behind them, the unfinished song was gaining. Sesshoshi seemed to know where he was going. He was headed in a straight path towards one of the blue doors.

The creature was almost right behind him now.

Sesshoshi burst through the door. Eiji looked over his shoulder again. The being had come to a stop at the threshold. In the dark space that seemed to hang before the beginning of a story, Eiji watch the creature sway in the doorway. Its androgynous face, still covered with bits of dirt, stared at her with its black eyes.

For a moment, as the creature looked at her, Eiji wondered if it was really she or the creature that was out of place in this world. Then the door shut and the creature was no longer a threat.

Eiji relaxed in Sesshoshi's arms. "I need to close my eyes."

"Hn." Was all she heard before she drifted off into the darkness.

Eiji awoke feeling warm and comfortable. *Am I dead?* Eiji wondered for a moment. She opened her eyes and found herself laying on a futon next to a small fire on the unearthed centre of a hut. She tried to sit up but sharp pain streaming from various parts of her body stopped her. Eiji raised her arms up for inspection. There were several cotton wraps around her arms. They were dark red with dried blood. She lifted up the blanket that was over her. She was naked. Eiji blushed. *The moon robe.* Where was it? Eiji looked around and located her clothing folded nearly on the floor. The moon robe was amongst them. Eiji sighed with relief and went back to inspecting her body.

Most of her body was covered with cotton wraps. Her back hurt the most. Now that she was out of her sleepy haze, the pain from the wound was sharp and constant.

Eiji looked from left to right. The hut she was in had no tatami mats. She was laying on a futon on the dirt floor. The floor had clearly been watered to keep the dust down. There were a few cooking utensils and bamboo baskets filled with fruit to her right. Her stomach growled at the sight of them.

Sesshoshi came through the door frame, carrying a pail of water.

His golden eyes fell on her immediately. "You are awake."

"So it would seem." Eiji smiled. The corners of his mouth twitched upwards. He knelt next to her and helped her sit up. Eiji kept the blanket in place around her chest. Sesshoshi handed her a cup of water and Eiji drank it quickly.

"How long was I asleep for?" Eiji asked.

"A couple of days."

Eiji's eye brows rose. "Hn."

Sesshoshi chuckled. "We are in Kobutori jii-san. There's not a lot of other characters in this story. The village is mostly empty even though there are several homes around. What kind of story is this?"

"It's a pretty simple one about selfishness. There's a kind old man and a mean one. They both have lumps on their cheeks. One man has a lump on the left cheek and the other on the right,"

Eiji said. She moved her hand to touch her cheek but she felt nothing.

"It is us. Some human commented on our lumps when I brought you into town."

"Ah. Anyway, the kind man goes into the mountains to get firewood but he falls asleep. When he wakes up there are yōkai sitting in a circle drinking sake and dancing. The old man is scared but he likes the dancing so he joins them. The yōkai like his dancing so they give him treasure and take his lump in exchange. The mean old man hears of this and heads into the mountain to find the yōkai. He dances for them but he does it so terribly and the yōkai become angry. They put the lump back on the right cheek. The mean old man returns home crying for being selfish." Eiji finished. She felt tired just from telling the story.

"Which one of us is the nice one?" Sesshoshi asked.

"Do you really want me to answer that?" Eiji laughed. She stopped her laughter short as pain shot through her ribs.

"Eiji. What happened with the unfinished being?" Sesshoshi asked. He brushed her hair away from her face. Eiji blushed. Her state of undress and Sesshoshi's gentle touches were taking her mind in a direction she couldn't go. Her body wouldn't like it if they were... physical. *So stop acting like it then,* she told her body.

Eiji pushed those thoughts to the back of her mind. "The unfinished beings. They can kill us for sure." Eiji told Sesshoshi about how the creature attacked her, her made up verses and her escape through the door.

She looked him in the eyes. "How did you know where to find me?"

"I waited for your return."

"I appeared right where it took me?"

Sesshoshi was quiet, he seemed to be thinking of something. "It was your blood. I could smell it."

Eiji nodded. "I see." His answer made sense but she had a nagging feeling that it wasn't the complete truth. She wanted to get dressed. "Sesshoshi, can you help me dress please? Just hand me my clothes and turn around." She was relieved when he didn't argue though he did give her a wicked smile before he put her clothes in her arms and turned his back. Once Eiji had secured her robe, she tucked the moon robe around her waist, hiding it.

"We should head up the mountain," Eiji said.

Sesshoshi chuckled and turned to face her. "Slow down. You still look pale and tired. We are in no rush."

"But this is the last story and then we'll be back home," Eiji said. "I'm sure our families will want to know where we are."

"Perhaps. But they can wait until you have recovered," Sesshoshi said. Eiji frowned but now that he mentioned it, she was feeling rather tired. Eiji sat back down on her futon, perhaps another nap by the fire would be alright. Eiji lay down and she was asleep as soon as she closed her eyes.

It took Eiji a few more days to feel like herself again. Once she was up to the task, they decided to head up into the mountains.

"We still haven't figured out which one of us is the nice one," Eiji said.

"We can ask which cheek our lumps are on," Sesshoshi said.

Eiji put out the fire in their hut. "Good idea." They headed outside. Eiji hadn't had a chance to look around the village. Sesshoshi had been right. There were plenty of huts but it seemed that the only inhabitants were those around their hut and the ones beyond were unoccupied. The village wasn't too different from the one in Hanasaka jiisan. The villagers wore cotton kimono and most looked like farmers.

A short, hunched woman walked by them. "Excuse me. Which cheek is my lump on?" Eiji asked her. The woman looked at Eiji for a moment before answering. "Your left." Then she continued on her way.

"That makes me the nice one, does it not?" Sesshoshi said.

"Yes but don't let it go to your head," Eiji said. Together they climbed the mountain. Eiji found a large tree near the top and settled down beneath it. "Can we rest for a moment?" She felt more like herself but she tired easily.

"Of course." Sesshoshi sat next to her and pulled her into his lap. Eiji's face felt hot. She still wasn't use to his affections though she thoroughly enjoyed them. She lay her head down on Sesshoshi's chest, nestling between his shoulder and the curve of his neck.

"I was afraid I had lost you."

Eiji's eyes widened at his admission. "I was afraid too. I didn't know how to defeat the creature or if there was even a way back to the Overworld. I haven't feared for my life like that in a long time."

"When was the last time you were afraid you would die? Was it when you first met me?"

Eiji smiled. "No. I was never scared of you."

He scoffed. "Sure, priestess." She knew he believed her. The moon robe hidden inside her kimono slid against her skin.

"Sesshoshi, what'll happen when we return?" Eiji asked.

She heard him sigh. "You have asked me that already."

"I know. I was hoping you had a clear answer this time," Eiji said.

"As I said before, I will not pretend nothing happened between us. But no one can see the future. I do not know what our relationship will look like after we return home," Sesshoshi said. Eiji nodded. She thought about the song she had made up to defeat the unfinished creature. *Sesshoshi, Sesshoshi, wolf in a cave. Backed by honour and doubt,* Eiji thought. *Who'll find you out?*

"Won't your family have issues with you –" Eiji searched for the right word. "Associating with a human?"

He was silent for a moment. "My mother might. My father will not. And I imagine Ko will be quite pleased." Eiji smiled at the thought of Lord Ko's face if they told him the two of them were an item. Sesshoshi kept talking. "My mother considers humans to be unintelligent, filthy and deceitful. When she was young, her father allowed humans to live on the palace grounds. I do not believe they treated her very well but she never speaks of the details."

"And your father?"

"He views humans as part of this world, neither good nor bad. However there is that rumour that the explorers from the west have brought the Emperor a weapon that can kill yōkai. It will level the playing field. Our strength and speed will not be enough of an advantage. My father wants to start improving relations between humans and yōkai before the weapon is made known," Sesshoshi said.

"So our relationship would be beneficial," Eiji said. Her voice sounded hollow to her own ears. Sesshoshi ran the back of his hand along her cheek.

"It would come at a rather opportune time. But that is not why I pursued you."

"You pursued me? I think I'm the one who went after you," Eiji said. When he chuckled she could hear it deep in his chest.

"You may think that if you wish."

Eiji snorted. She smiled to herself and closed her eyes. Eiji still felt as if their relationship would be a burden on Sesshoshi. *I could make him forget with the moon robe. If it works, that is.* Eiji thought. She would remember and she would miss him, their conversations, his touch, but it would be her burden alone.

Sesshoshi said nothing further and so Eiji slept for a while in his arms. She woke up when she heard the sounds of a crackling fire and loud voices singing joyful songs.

Eiji opened her eyes. "The yōkai are here."

"I know. I heard them arrive a while ago."

"You should have woken me up," Eiji said.

"You still need to rest. We are in no rush," Sesshoshi said. "The yōkai have only just arrived." Eiji slid out of his lap, immediately feeling the loss of his warmth. Together they moved toward the festive yōkai. They emerged from the forest into a large clearing. Red and blue yōkai sat in a circle drinking rice wine and singing. One of the yōkai was in the centre of the circle dancing while the others clapped and cheered him on.

Eiji smiled but her smile dropped off her face when she saw the look in Sesshoshi's eyes.

"What's wrong?" Eiji asked.

"Is this really how humans see us?" he said.

Eiji looked at the yōkai once again. They were brightly coloured, unlike any yōkai she had encountered in her life. Their muscles were disproportionate, large in some areas and small in others. They looked like an exaggeration, like how yōkai were described in stories. *Obviously,* Eiji thought, remembering where she was.

"In some ways, yes. But humans know what real higher yōkai look like. I think these kinds of representations are hyperbole of the lower yōkai that attack us more often," Eiji said.

Sesshoshi continued to look like he had eaten sour tofu. "It is embarrassing."

"It's not real," Eiji said but she felt for him.

"Hn."

Eiji sighed. "There's no use in staring, you have to get in there and dance with them." She was hoping Sesshoshi would dance for real. It would be a sight to remember, she was sure. He said nothing before he moved towards the clearing. He breezed by the yōkai and began to dance. Well, it was a kind of a dance. Eiji recognized the movements as the mantras they had practised during their training together, only Sesshoshi was doing them much faster.

Eiji felt her heart twist. Not only was she now certain that she had looked like a monkey wearing a geisha's geta while doing the mantras, Eiji was falling for Sesshoshi even more. His face looked stoic but his eyes were full of emotion. Eiji felt like a fool for ever having thought he was emotionless. His eyes were full of concentration, pride, desire.

Eiji blushed. It was desire for her.

She remembered their conversation from earlier. Sesshoshi had said their relationship would have come at an opportune time but that this was not the reason why he had grown fond of her. She believed him though her mind nagged at her that it was too good to be true. The moon robe shifted against her skin. Would she want to forget him? To forget their time together? It would save her the pain that might come from his rejection of her when they returned to their world. Eiji didn't think he would turn away from her because he had been lying, but she worried about how he would react when actually faced with the realities of a human-yōkai relationship in the public eye. The very public eye. He was the yōkai lord of the western lands after all. That was easy to forget when his hands were on her, when he kissed her. If she had laid hands on him in their world she would have been dead before her finger tips brushed his skin. If not by Sesshoshi's hand, then by any other yōkai that would have witnessed it. Eiji would never be safe. She didn't want to inconvenience him by forcing him into the role of her protector.

Eiji would be making him choose constantly. Between human and yōkai kind, between his family's honour and his love for her, between his time defending his lands and time spent with her. These kinds of thoughts tumbled around in her mind like a wave breaking on the shore.

But then she watched him move. The way his claws swiped through the air, the way his shoulders shifted, the way his hair floated behind him every time he changed position. Eiji wanted him, but she didn't want to burden him.

By the time he finished his so-called dance, she had decided.

Chapter 16

When Sesshoshi finished moving through the mantras the
yōkai applauded him. He looked over to where Eiji stood.
Something about her had changed. Perhaps she was still tired
from her injuries.

"Superb!"

"Magnificent!" Shouted the yōkai. Sesshoshi turned his
attention back to them. He bowed to them and the yōkai clapped
even more.

"You must come back and dance for us again. Take this
treasure. We'll hold onto that lump on your face. I'm sure you'll
want it back. Come dance for us again and we'll return it to you,"
one of the red yōkai said. He approached Sesshoshi and ran his
chunky hand along Sesshoshi's cheek.

Sesshoshi left the yōkai and returned to Eiji's side.

She smiled up at him but there was a hint of sadness in
her eyes. "That was beautiful."

"Hn. Let us find a suitable place to sleep for the night."
Sesshoshi moved through the woods until they found a stretch of
mossy ground.

Eiji looked down at the moss. "I miss my futon already."

Sesshoshi chuckled. "Understandable." He settled down
onto the moss. The night was warm and dry so the moss was not
unpleasant to lay on. Sesshoshi grabbed Eiji's wrist and pulled
her down beside him. She sat beside him and leaned against him,
melding into his side.

"What is going on inside your mind? You have been
troubled since this morning," Sesshoshi said. He heard her sigh.

"Nothing."

"You are lying."

Another sigh, this one angry. "Fine. I'm worried about
what things will be like when we return home."

"That is understandable," Sesshoshi said. Eiji looked up at
him. It was clear by the way her face twisted that his answer was

not acceptable.

"Really? Nothing else to say?" Eiji frowned.

"I am not sure what I could say. I do not know what it will be like so I can not tell you. And I am not as worried about it as you are," Sesshoshi said.

"You're not? What about your family? What about the way my father will react?" Eiji asked.

"How will they react?"

"They'll – Um, I don't know. They'll probably be mad," Eiji said.

"See, you do not know either," Sesshoshi said and tapped her forehead affectionately. "So there is no point in worrying about it."

"I guess," Eiji said. He knew she had not relaxed a bit from his words. Eiji slid her hand along her waist, along the spot where the moon robe lay. Sesshoshi was certain she thought he did not know she had it, but she was wrong. He had seen her take it. He was not sure why she had taken it. The kimono was pretty but it did not seem special in any other way.

"Are you worried your moon robe will not make it back with you?" Sesshoshi asked. He was growing tired of her secrecy.

Eiji gasped. "How did you know about that?" She sounded angry again. *Fair enough. I would be too if I felt like I could never hide anything,* Sesshoshi thought.

"I saw you take it and I found it on you when I was patching you up. Besides it makes your waist twice as thick. Did you think I would not notice that?" Sesshoshi said with a predatory grin. Eiji blushed.

"I took it from the moon people just before we left Kaguya's story."

"But why?" Sesshoshi asked.

"It looked so beautiful. I'd read about the robe from the story. I've never had anything so nice before," Eiji said. Sesshoshi was satisfied with her answer though he knew she was holding back. He had to allow her to have her secrets. Sesshoshi ran his hand along her back and sides until Eiji drifted off to sleep. He closed his eyes and slept as well.

The next evening, the yōkai had gathered again, singing

and dancing in the clearing.

Eiji took a deep breath and huffed. "I feel embarrassed already."

Sesshoshi chuckled. "I am the only one who will really be watching."

"Exactly." She joined the yōkai in the clearing and moved through the mantras just as Sesshoshi had the day before. He smiled at her performance. Eiji had come a long way since the beginning of their training but she was nowhere near as precise and skilful as someone who had trained their entire life as he had. When she finished the yōkai yelled at her. Sesshoshi frowned. He knew it was part of the story but Eiji's sensitive nature made her hurt at their words. Sesshoshi disliked the look forming on her face.

"That was terrible. Take your lump back and be gone," a blue yōkai said. He moved his hand across Eiji's cheek, presumably putting the lump back on her other cheek. In the story it should mean that Eiji now had two lumps, one on each cheek, though Sesshoshi could not see them.

Eiji returned to his side. Her eyes were watering. "At least it's easy to make me cry."

"That is not a good thing," Sesshoshi said. She smiled slightly.

Through the thick of the trees Sesshoshi could see a white light emerging. "The door is over there." Eiji looked up and saw it as well. They reached the door in no time and pushed through it. They were back in the Overworld once again. Sesshoshi squinted as his eyes adjusted to the bright expanse.

"Look! A tori gate," Eiji said. Before them was a huge tori gate. It towered high above their heads. Sesshoshi could not look at it all at once. It was surrounded by doors of colours Sesshoshi had never seen. He thought about what Granny had told them in the story of Momotaro. The short cut would take them here faster and they would never find their way out if they tried to find the doors on their own. She had been right. *It might have taken me years to find this place on my own,* Sesshoshi thought.

"We'll return to our world when we pass through right?" Eiji asked. He could sense her hesitation. It was similar to his own.

"Only one way to find out," Sesshoshi said. He turned to Eiji and lifted her chin. He placed a soft kiss on her lips. "Do not worry about what will happen in the future." Eiji said nothing but nodded. Sesshoshi walked through the tori gate with Eiji close on his heels. A bright light engulfed them. He felt something smooth and silky settle over his shoulders. His eyes widened. *The moon robe. What is she –*

Sesshoshi blinked. He watched Eiji, standing across from him, tug the red scroll out of his hands. What had they just been doing? He could not remember. He continued to stare into her brown eyes and she stared back. Something odd had happened, he could tell but he did not know what. The way Eiji looked at him was vastly different from any way she had ever looked at him before. He could tell she was trying to work something out in her head.

Finally she spoke. "P– please Sesshoshi. Let me keep this scroll. You can have the rest."

Right. They had come to collect fairytales for Lord Ko. Eiji had told him not to touch this one. He realized that she had just called him Sesshoshi without his proper title. He had killed for less but the urge to spill blood was not in him. The sound of his name on her lips stirred him in a way he had never felt before. She had said it in such a familiar way.

"Lord Sesshoshi," he corrected. It was an automatic response.

"Sorry my Lord," Eiji said. She placed the red scroll in a scabbard and put in on her grandmother's futon. "Please Lord Sesshoshi let me keep it." She had already put it away. Sesshoshi was sure she thought he would not object. He searched his emotions. He could not deny her.

"Fine. Lord Ko will have plenty of stories with the others," Sesshoshi said.

"Yes my Lord," Eiji said. Her formal answers bothered him.

He realized that the sun was low. It was later in the day than he had remembered. He left without saying another word. There was a feeling he could not shake. Eiji was deceiving him, but how and about what? He returned to the western palace in a daze. As he headed down the corridor, Ritsuka appeared in his path.

"Oh Lord Sesshoshi. You have returned." Ritsuka smiled at him. It annoyed him, more than usual.

"I am on my way to see Lord Ko," he said. Ritsuka pouted but said nothing further. He wanted to get away from her as fast as possible. This female was not right for him. He nearly stopped mid-step, did that mean that he knew which female was? He growled. That human priestess had bewitched him. What had she done? It bothered him for the rest of the day and by nightfall he was no closer to the answer. Eventually he slept.

Sesshoshi awoke from a dream. He and Eiji were training in a clearing. She had been using her scythe and he his sword. They had not gotten far into their training before he had pulled her to him. Then, Sesshoshi smirked at the images that replayed in his mind. Eiji was as responsive a lover as she was a person. Her expressions pleased him and her noises stirred something deep within him, a possessiveness he only expected to experience for a chosen mate.

He paused. Usually the thought of laying with a human would have repulsed him but his dream of Eiji had done the opposite. *The Tale of the Bamboo Cutter.* The words flashed through his mind. It was a name of one of the fairytale Sesshoshi had seen the day before. Then he remembered an old childless couple, in fact he remembered several old childless couples. Sesshoshi's eyes widened slightly. His dream. He knew now that it was a memory.

He clenched his fist. Eiji. He had been right. Something had happened between them. Eiji must have done something to make him forget. He could not remember everything, just bits and pieces though he felt that soon all his memories would return. Sesshoshi frowned but then he grinned.

Eiji might be as cunning as a fox yōkai, but Sesshoshi was remembering. When all of his memories returned he would pay Eiji a little visit.

Author's note

Thank you for reading. I hope you enjoyed my first novel and will consider leaving a review. The Priestess and Yōkai II is available now! If you find any errors in this book and wish to report them please email <u>lindseymerril@gmail.com</u>.

Until next time!